The Circumcision

GYÖRGY DALOS

Translated by Judith Sollosy

MARION BOYARS
LONDON • NEW YORK

This book is dedicated to
Katinka Mezei and Michael Köcher in Vienna,
Katalin Katz in Jerusalem,
and Marius Tabacun in Cluj Napoca
György Dalos

The translation is lovingly dedicated
to my parents Joseph and Elizabeth Sollosy
and my lovely sister Klara
Judith Sollosy

1

IN THE YEAR 5716*, as the month of *Tevet*** was drawing to a close, Robi Singer was heading home over Stalin Bridge on the crowded Number 33 tram. He was despondent. *Shabbes**** was over, it had 'gone out' as they said in the orphanage, so he could ride the tram without having to feel guilty. Nonetheless, he wished it were spring, the month of *Iyyar* or *Nisan*, for instance, because then it would be light around five o'clock and still *Shabbes*, and he'd have to cross Stalin Bridge on foot and continue along Váci Road on foot, all the way to Marx Square.

With the approach of spring, Mr Balla exacted a promise from his charges – the half-orphaned, and the fully orphaned who had grandparents waiting for them at home – to honour *Shabbes*. It's not such a big thing for a twelve-year-old to get on a tram when he isn't permitted to, he explained, but small sins lead to big sins, the pardonable

---

* In the Jewish calendar, years are counted not from the birth of Christ, but from the creation of the world, which is thought to have happened in 3761 BC. So the Jewish year 5716 is equivalent to 1955 in the Roman calendar.

** The Jewish calendar is lunar based and as the lunar year is approximately 354 days while a solar year is 365 days, an extra month is inserted into the lunar calendar every few years to adjust it to the solar year. The names of the months are Babylonian in origin, and commence in the first month, Passover. *Nisan*: March - April; *Iyyar*: April - May; *Sivan*: May - June; *Tammuz*: June - July; *Av*: July - August; *Elul*: August - September; *Tishrei*: September - October; *Cheshvan*: October - November; *Kislev*: November - December; *Tevet*: December - January; *Shevat*: January - February; *Adar*: February - March.

*** Hebrew. A colloquial derivative for '*Shabbat*', the weekly day of rest which begins on Friday at sunset and lasts until nightfall on Saturday.

to the unpardonable. 'A Jew must honour the *Shabbes* even on a desert island,' he explained. 'Had Robinson been *unsereiner,* one of us,' he went on, 'in all probability he'd have called the fine savage that joined up with him Saturday instead of Friday, and would have used him as a *Shabbes goy,** for man is never left to fend for himself, he's never short on divine charity.'

They had a *Shabbes goy* at the orphanage, too, a former maid from Transylvania they called Aunt Marie. On Friday night when the boys went to bed, it was her job to turn out the light. As soon as she left the dormitory, though, the boys would flick the light switch on and off, out of mischief, as if to see what the Lord would have to say to such colossal impudence.

The Lord, however, said nothing, unless, of course, you're willing to concede that when the forty-watt bulb gave off a sizzle and burned itself out because of all that switching on and off, it was His way of expressing His anger – which is what Balla thought.

'See? I told you,' he said the next morning when Gábor Blum heroically took the mischief upon himself. 'This is the Lord's way of punishing those donkeys who'd like to try His infinite patience with such cheap pranks.'

ON THIS PARTICULAR winter's afternoon, though, when it grew dark early, Robi Singer could ride the tram with a clear conscience, and a good thing it was, too, because it was freezing outside. Robi Singer shivered as he wrapped his short coat, worn over his blue sweater, more tightly around him. His grandmother called the short, light-weight coat 'transitional', which sounded promising. Now and then on the weekend, his mother or grandmother would even say, 'One of these days we will buy you a real winter

---

* A non-Jewish person who carries out work, prohibited for orthodox Jews, during the Shabbat.

coat, dear,' or more cautiously, 'You could use a real winter coat, dear.'

Grandmother was ticking off the days to the deadline for the new winter coat at the next bonus time, when her unselfish devotion to the cause as an unskilled worker would surely be noticed. Unfortunately, the reshufflings, rationalisations and mergers in vogue at the time prevented Grandmother from being in any one place long enough. First she was transferred from the Rain and Trench Coat Co-operative to the Hat and Headgear Co-operative, and then, most recently, from the Hat and Headgear Co-operative to the Kerchief Dyers' Co-operative without enough time to warm her feet in either place.

Nonetheless, Robi Singer believed in the bonus, just as he believed that the day would come when Grandmother would take him by the hand and they'd go to the Department Store for Reduced Goods. There they would finally put an end to this state of transition, which had been in transition for so long, it was no longer a transition at all. Let the sub-zero temperatures rage and the high winds howl, throwing twelve-year-olds like himself against the ancient gates of Óbuda.

Winter would be helpless against his wonderfully warm brand-new winter coat.

That winter was exceptionally cold, the coldest in Robi Singer's memory. The state school announced a two-week coal recess, and the orphanage, too, was afflicted by a chronic lack of heating fuel. In the morning, the boys crowded into two rooms, where their teachers tried to keep them busy. They had to chop up the ping-pong tables in order to have kindling for the stoves. Balla tried to console his charges by reminding them that while the *goys* were just as cold as they were, in *Eretz Yisroel** it was nice and warm and people were running around in their shirt sleeves.

Some comfort, Robi Singer thought, when the orphanage

---

* The Land of Israel.

food was also going from bad to worse. As far as he was concerned, in this respect the *goys* definitely had the advantage over them. They could eat bacon and cheese, and on Sunday even pork chops. Whereas the boys at the orphanage had to make do with miserly portions of beef served in all its imaginable variations, the kosher sausage being as appealing as it got. If only their portions weren't the size of a thumb-nail. They barely lasted through prayers. The *scholet** had more barley in it than beans, the holiday chicken stew had more onions than chicken, and the morning's malt coffee was not just lukewarm, but tasted foul into the bargain.

Balla explained eagerly to anyone willing to listen how on the one hand all of this was Hitler's fault and the fault of his mad war. On the other hand, it was the international situation, which affected them directly, seeing that the frontiers were closed, and the Joint** couldn't support the orphanage properly.

'Still,' he continued, 'we will not eat *trayf*,*** we haven't come to that. In worse times than these, the people of Israel survived as a people by adherence to custom. In the desert,' he went on, 'who'd have ever considered satisfying his hunger with unclean pork stew, thinking only about his stomach when the survival of the Jews was at stake?'

Though Robi Singer tended to agree with his tutor's reasoning, he found it wanting all the same. For instance,

---

* A Sabbath stew made of white beans, barley and smoked brisket or of breast or leg of goose. As the Sabbath is a day of rest, all Saturday meals have to be cooked ahead of time, as it is forbidden to light a fire. The *scholet* was cooked slowly in an oven that was lit on Friday before dusk, so it would still be hot for Saturday lunch.

** *Abbrev.* American Joint Distribution Committee, formed in 1915 to join together the Jewish Reform, Conservative and Orthodox movements to provide relief for European Jewry. It was most active in helping Jewish Holocaust survivors resettle to the USA, Australia and Canada after the War.

*** Yiddish, *lit.* 'torn'. Non-kosher food. From the Hebrew *trefah*, which is any food that is forbidden by Jewish law.

at times, necessity posed a real threat to custom. Take *Sukkot*, for instance, when there were at most five of the prescribed fifteen kinds of fruit on the long dining-room table, and of the five, three were stewed fruit from the Globus Canning Factory. Dates and figs and oranges were soaking up the golden sun in far-off Israel, he had no problem with that. But where were the apples, pears and walnuts for the orphanage table?

AS HE WAS heading home, though, it was not the occasional snags in Balla's dialectics that preoccupied Robi Singer. On weekends, his mind turned to thoughts of the warm tiled stove and the more generous helping of food waiting for him at home. He also relished the magical change in the environment which he compared to what he'd seen at the Youth Theatre, thanks to a prize ticket from the state school. In the semi-darkness between scenes, Robi reasoned, the castle turns into a forest, but the stage remains the stage. Likewise, as *Shabbes* faded into the distance, so did the venue of his life, even if life itself remained the same. Instead of Óbuda, Pest; instead of the crowded dormitories, the high-ceilinged, two-room apartment in Terézváros; instead of the institution camp bed, the large divan which he shared with Grandmother; instead of the white night stand, the sideboard with its hidden recesses, and in the drawer of the sewing machine Grandmother had on loan from the Synagogue, the select table-soccer team which was waiting for him, too, even if some of the players had been removed by Grandmother now and then for household purposes. And the world outside! The bakeries on the Grand Boulevard redolent

---

* The feast of the Tabernacles which commemorates the wanderings of the Children of Israel when they dwelt in huts or booths. It is also observed as a thanksgiving holy day for the bounties of nature during the previous year – a harvest festival.

with the scent of coffee and caramels, one forint thirty for the *mignons* and one forty for the cream puffs, the Torchbearer cinema with its Russian war films and fresh pretzels, and on Saturday night, listening to their recently bought People's Radio broadcasting a variety show – entertainment-value guaranteed by the state. At such times Grandmother turned out the light, partly to economise, and partly, as she jokingly put it, to heighten the effect of all that culture.

But there was something Robi Singer was not looking forward to. He was not looking forward to his mother opening the door for him. Mother always greeted him with too much enthusiasm, her embrace too tense, her kisses too wet. She gave Robi the most preposterous pet names, which she insisted on using even in the presence of strangers. In her search for yet another name for him, she had practically exhausted the entire animal kingdom, until Grandmother came to the rescue.

'The child is not a lap dog,' she said disapprovingly. 'Can't you just call him by his name?'

Saturday night to Sunday night, Robi Singer was busy dodging Mother's kisses and embraces. Grandmother was different, though. She had no need for such effusive displays of affection. She knew how to love with her eyes. Her glance fell on her grandson at a slight angle, and from above. Once in a while, she'd praise Robi's high forehead or clean, honest eyes, but even when most taken with him, she would simply say, 'The boy is the spitting image of his father,' praise that Robi could acknowledge without the blood rushing to his cheeks.

Robi also liked going for walks with Grandmother, and shopping with her. 'She sees people and merchandise for what they are,' he thought appreciatively. 'When we run into friends and she stops for a quick chat, they look so honoured.' She walked so fast and with such self-assurance, Robi could hardly keep up with her.

On the other hand, due to a congenital dislocation of her hip, Mother walked with a limp. Every step she took was precarious, and she would often wait for the third green light before getting the nerve to cross the street. She'd also gained a lot of weight in the last couple of years, and now when she walked, she pressed one of her oversize handbags to her left bosom, like a shield. This is how – limping, shielding herself with her oversize handbag – she proceeded every Sunday morning, to the Brotherhood of Jews for Christ. Reluctantly giving in to Grandmother's pleas, Robi Singer went with her. Mother needed to be escorted because, apart from her numerous other ailments, she was agoraphobic and was afraid of the stairs. She was scared she would fall. But the only way to enter or leave their second-floor apartment was by the stairs. Even the Brotherhood's prayer hall has a couple of steps.

On Sunday morning, Robi had an hour and a half between the two sets of stairs, enough time to go home and wait for Mother to make her hesitant, limping way back from prayers, then call up to him from under their window. But Robi knew that Mother would call out for him, using one of his many pet names, and to prevent this, he would rather sit in the warm prayer room, reading the New Testament or a book of psalms, casting anxious looks at Mother – who kept dozing off during the sermon, to be startled awake by the sound of the harmonium and the congregation striking up the song, 'Lamb of God, who art upon yonder Golgotha' – or at Uncle Izidor Reiter, the leader of the congregation, who made his way between the rows, handing out wine and wafers, his eyes on the lookout for a believer willing to give public testimony to their faith.

'Go on, dear,' Grandmother would say around nine-thirty on Sunday morning, 'go on, if you must. I'll make you lunch. Have a nice pray. It'll improve your appetite.'

If there was one thing that Mother didn't need, it was to improve her appetite with the aid of Jewish-Christian prayer. Afflicted as she was with a dislocation of the hip, agoraphobia and, in order of appearance, lung, liver and gall bladder complaints, obsessional neurosis and chronic insomnia – sixteen ailments in all by Robi's last count – Mother seemed to concentrate all her remaining life-force on satisfying her hunger. Beginning with the morning's four slices of bread with jam and butter, followed by a cup of hot cocoa at ten, the ample potato or pasta lunches, and the biscuits and scones she always had on hand, all she did was eat and eat and eat, despite doctor's orders to restrain herself. But the pleasure of eating was not complete without Mother's superstitious ritual of medicine-taking. What's more, because she was afraid she'd end up poisoning herself with the tranquillisers, medicinal charcoals, antacids, analgesics, laxatives, sedatives and occasional antipyrines and aspirins, she refused to take her medicines except in the presence of a witness.

IN THE MORNING Robi Singer's mother would drag herself out of her cramped domain, the smaller of their two rooms, with a cloying cloud of medicinal vapours and the heavy odour of night-sweat trailing behind her. Her face, puffy from sleeping pills, or insomnia, or both, looked like it'd been given a going-over by a thug. Her thinning hair, the colour of poppy-seeds, clung helplessly to her scalp, and her eyes stared unseeing into the world, so that she used her arms to grope her way to the toilet. Still, nothing alarmed Robi Singer as much as Mother's weight, because it reminded him of himself.

For her part, Grandmother thought of Robi's obesity as one of the seven wonders of the world. The generous doses of vitamin shots – a present from the American people – jump-started the spectacular process of amplification that turned the puny, prematurely born child into the uncontested champion of the weight-gaining Olympics sponsored by the

Jewish World Congress at the children's home in Zugliget. The noteworthy championship was written up by a Zionist journal in London, and someone sent the photo-report, with a rough translation, to Grandmother. According to the enthusiastic account, the then four-year-old and very obese Robi Singer – 'little Bob' in the original – was living proof of the vitality of the Chosen People and their determination to survive.

Robi was far less enthusiastic about his tenacious celebrity. He was ashamed of the softness of his body, his fist-sized breasts, his drooping behind and the nickname of 'Fatso', which stuck to him like molasses as he moved from one children's home to another. He was ashamed of his body, a prison of fat, and his obese, wobbling mother. He would have liked to hide from the eyes of the world. Often he felt that another person dwelt inside him, a lean, tall, muscular other who walked the streets of Budapest with his beautiful young mother. They would be proud of each other, too, but without making a show of it, for nothing is more natural than being handsome, and being neither too fat nor too thin, but exactly as you should be.

After such vain daydreams came the bitter awakening to the true proportions of his body and the image of himself indelibly stamped in his memory, which he could see from the outside, as it were. With his limping mother by his side, they attempt to cross with the green light to the other side of the *Oktogon*⃰. It's the third time the light's turned green, and though he's trying to convince himself that he'd have crossed ages ago were he by himself, the passers-by see two helpless, obese human beings intimidated by the light traffic on the square. The younger one takes the older by the arm, the boy takes his mother's arm as they head into the glaring light of their mutual shame. Surely, when Grandmother praises his high forehead and clear, honest eyes, or says that he's 'the

---

⃰ A busy octagonal shaped square in central Budapest at the intersection of two major boulevards.

spitting image of his father', she's just trying to console him out of the goodness of her heart, or so Robi Singer thinks.

THE FACT IS that Robi Singer's father, Andor Singer, was an exceptional man who spoke several languages, and whose real field was supposed to have been art history. He never made it, though, because prior to the war Jews couldn't finish university, as Robi's grandmother explained. Thus, it is not quite clear to Robi how or when Father could have practised the discipline of art history, in which he was such a pro that all his friends and acquaintances sang his praises. Grandmother pronounced the words 'art history' softly, like a prayer, and made no secret of her dearest wish – that one day, when he grew up, her grandson should major in art history, too. 'You will succeed,' she'd say, 'where our poor Bandika failed.' Still, despite his multitude of talents, 'our poor Bandika' was a *Pechvogel**, a fact that even Grandmother's indulgent stories could not hide.

The gravest and last stroke of bad luck caught up with Robi's father right after the liberation, during the month of *Elul* of the year 5706, when the insidious disease that had attacked his lungs carried him off.

'My poor son-in-law,' Grandmother said, 'was taken from us by galloping consumption.' To satisfy Robi Singer's curiosity, she even told him the place of his death, St John's Hospital. Not considering this information precise enough, she added the mysterious words, 'Poor Bandika died in Walnut Ditch.' In various petitions and applications, which Grandmother was a real pro at composing, she put it differently, saying that her son-in-law fell 'a victim to fascism'.

Grandmother also said that the greatest and final stroke of bad luck in this tragedy was the fact that soon after Robi's father died, Dr Fleming's life-saving discovery, penicillin,

---

* Yiddish, *colloq*. An unfortunate person, a 'no-hoper'.

became widely available in Europe.

'My poor son-in-law,' Grandmother said. 'If only he'd waited a month, he'd still be with us today.'

There was no knowing who this hidden reproach was aimed at – the dearly departed who should have known better and waited, Dr Fleming, who should have been quicker about it, or the Lord God, whom Grandmother suspected was behind this thing, and who allowed it happen.

Robi Singer, who did not know that Walnut Ditch was a street name, often imagined his father lying in a ditch the first summer after the war, waiting in vain for Dr Fleming, who'd already crossed the ocean with his hypodermic needle and was heading straight for Hungary. Robi Singer concluded that since the consequences of Dr Fleming's belated appearance could not be remedied, he'd do as his grandmother suggested, grow up and study art history, so he could prove in the face of Fate that there was still justice in the world.

IN SHORT, Robi Singer dreamed of a career in art history. But as he did so, he also felt an ever-growing interest in another kind of history, the history of the Jewish people, which could hardly be called art, unless – as Balla said – you considered survival as a form of art. It was Balla who awakened his curiosity in Jewish history when, between two Bible classes (and only on a voluntary basis, of course), he began recounting tales of the latter-day history of the Jews, stories that you could not find in the Bible. On Balla's lips the greatest heroes, Judas Maccabeus, Akiba and Bar Kochba, all came to life, and with them, the latter-day heroes of the Warsaw Ghetto and the pioneers of *Eretz Yisroel*. They were all strong and courageous and unlikely to carry extra pounds on them, and when they died – because many of them died – it wasn't due to a stroke of bad luck, but to their heroic determination, the earnest desire to wash away the shameful badge of cowardice from the face of their nation.

'They have died,' Balla said, 'and their bodies lie mouldering in the cold earth, but their souls stand guard over what's left of the Chosen People. We must do all we can to be worthy of them.'

How one was supposed to be worthy of someone, Robi Singer had no idea. But Balla's words stuck to him like iron shavings stick to a magnet. Dates, names, concrete events, quotations from poems – they stuck deep and they stuck fast.

In the early days of the month of *Tevet*, when the great fuel shortage hit the orphanage and the iron stove in the small auditorium crackled softly from the slivers of what had been the ping-pong table, Balla suggested a new game.

'I want each of you to pick the name of a great Jewish hero, someone you would like to be.' The biblical names came quick and fast, Abrahams and Moseses, Jacobs and Mordechais, names the boys knew from Bible class. Except, this time Balla was curious to know how many of the Hebrew names that he had taught his charges they could remember. Last time, for instance, he told them stories about Bar Kochba, the Son of the Star, who fought heroically and successfully for years against the Romans, until he fell in battle.

Robi Singer realised that Bar Kochba was the name Balla wanted to hear. When his tutor cast a disappointed glance around the room, as if to say that the seed he had planted apparently did not fall on fertile soil, Robi put up his hand and, blushing to the roots of his hair, announced his claim to the Bar Kochba name. Smoothing back his chestnut-brown hair, Balla sighed with relief, and a joyful gleam danced in his eye.

'I've been watching you, Singer,' he said, 'you're a natural born historian.'

From then on, Balla spent at least half an hour with Robi

every day. He called Robi to the teacher's room, told him about Jewish history and questioned him. What's more, half in jest and half in earnest, during these sessions, Balla called Robi Ben Bar Kochba, the Son of the Son of the Star. Robi Singer shivered ecstatically every time.

Still, as he was now heading home on the Number 33 tram, Robi Singer's mind was otherwise engaged. The cause was yesterday's meeting with Balla. Oddly enough, it had been arranged for a Friday, just before the lighting of the candles took place, when Balla was always flat out. It was no time for him to talk about history, and he didn't. Balla, who was sitting by his desk, asked Robi to take a seat on the ottoman under an oil-print of Moses Mendelssohn.*

'Look here, son,' he began, pausing, then launching into it again. 'In short, son,' he said, clearing his throat.

Between Balla's two attempts at addressing him, Robi Singer had plenty of time to feel a surge of excitement.

'Dear Robi,' Balla said, now for the third time, obviously determined to go through with what he had to say, 'You will be thirteen years old next year. Have you considered your Bar Mitzvah?'

'I have,' Robi Singer said, turning as white as a sheet.

'In that case, consider it some more,' Balla said, a faint smile appearing in the corner of his eye. 'Which reminds me,' he went on, his voice more firm this time, indicating that he was about to reveal the reason why he'd ordered Robi Singer to his room, 'It's high time you were circumcised.'

ROBI SINGER'S ANXIETY that it would be his mother who'd open the door for him was unfounded. As he walked up the stairs, he saw that the kitchen window was covered with an impenetrable layer of steam. Robi realised that it

---

* German Jewish philosopher (1729-1786) who opened up secular learning for German Jews and was instrumental in fighting for full equality for the Jews of Europe.

was one of those Saturday afternoons when Grandmother did the pre-wash. Before taking the bedlinen to the State Laundry on Monday morning, she subjected it to a thorough scrutiny, and if she found any suspicious-looking stains or discolouration, the linen was soaked in a basin filled with boiling water, then wrung out and hung on the clothesline. The women working at the State Laundry couldn't praise Grandmother's love of clean linen enough. Once the woman who took in her laundry even said, so the customer next in line behind Grandmother could hear, 'See? This is what I call dirty linen.'

When she did the soaking, Grandmother usually sent Mother on a walk. 'Go on, dear, take a breath of fresh air,' she'd say, though all she really wanted was to get her out of the way. This time, though, Mother didn't have to be told. She came home from the Bureau for Textile Exports, grabbed a bite of her re-heated lunch, and went off on her usual health rounds.

Mother was bound by close, one might even say intimate, ties to the medical community of Pest. Now that she'd been put on partial disability and she had to work just four hours a day at the Bureau for Textile Exports, she spent nearly every afternoon at the Union Health Centre. She 'toddled along', as Grandmother put it, to the Csengery Street branch, left her winter coat in the cloakroom, asked at the desk for numbers for the numerous lines she wished to join, then tickets in hand, made her way to the specialists. She generally started at Neurology, proceeding to Dentistry, Rheumatology, Dermatology and Internal Medicine, with Optometry being the latest addition to her list. In each of these places the doctors and nurses greeted her as an old friend, and if she couldn't discharge her duty towards every one of her illnesses because, for instance, she happened to suffer from a mild cold, they'd remark lightly, 'Have you forgotten us so soon?' Mother gladly put up with the long lines and the often painful medical procedures, for on these

Saturday afternoons she was generously compensated by being, if only for a moment or two, the centre of attention.

And, as Robi Singer knew from accompanying his mother, there was a real club-like atmosphere at the Csengery Street centre. As they waited on the long white benches, people would exchange detailed descriptions of their illnesses and, during influenza season, when a coughing crowd wrapped in shawls flooded the information desk, it was like a public holiday. Test results, prescriptions and patients' records appeared as if by miracle from behind the small dispensary windows, and the enigmatic light of the X-ray room came filtering through half-opened changing-room doors. Breaking through the waiting crowd, two medics rolled a parchment-skinned woman to surgery. This was Mother's intimate world, inhabited by the idolized overseers of her illnesses, a good number of whom she fell in love with through the years, sometimes more than one at the same time.

ONCE A WEEK, Mother's health rounds ended in the room marked 'Psychotherapy', where Dr Nádai treated what was left of his pre-war clientele. Dr Nádai, the respected psychotherapist, was well on in years and hard of hearing, but out of humanitarian considerations he was allowed to keep practising a profession which in the meantime had become suspect. He listened to Mother's complaints with the smooth routine of a man who had fifty years of understanding and empathy behind him. He made few comments; at most, he'd nod now and then. It seemed, however, that this nodding was enough for Mother, who continued seeing Dr Nádai in the small 'mental hygiene' cubicle wedged in between Cardiology and Gastroenterology.

But Mother got something else from the old psychiatrist besides understanding nods. A couple of years ago, he gave her an official signed document to the effect that Mrs Andor

F/2038749

Singer named therein, now widowed, was suffering from severe neurosis, was under his care, and needed 'complete rest and quiet'. Robi Singer never once saw his mother show this testimony to anyone, but he knew that she kept it among her most prized possessions, including photographs of her son, sometimes rereading the nearly illegible expert opinion with great relish.

Neurosis – this was the basis of all the illnesses that filled Mother's daily life. The word needed no explanation. Simple and mysterious, its weight spoke for itself. At times, Robi Singer's mother used the adjective 'serious' in conjunction with it, and, at rare intervals, even the word *gravis*, its Latin equivalent. It was only on the rarest occasion that she'd allow Dr Nádai's serious-sounding diagnosis of *neurasthenia anancastica gravis* to pass her lips. The Greek word in the middle made her proud, for it meant that she was in no way responsible for the nature of the illness that afflicted her.

IT WAS INDEED a grave moment when one day Mother was fired from her work at the Office Machine Marketing Company. Dr Nádai gave her the official document, partly to ease the shock. The reason given for her dismissal was the trend for job 'rationalisation'. Actually, it was nice of the management to keep the real, embarrassing reason for Mother's dismissal discreetly under cover, and make no mention of the fact that within two months of her starting work, she had forgotten how to type. Still, this did nothing to alter the fact that Mother felt she had been kicked out. When, having picked up her personal file from Personnel, she reached the stairs, she became dizzy and realised she would never make it down. For a while she stood around anxiously, but then went back to Personnel, where weeping, she begged them that if they must get rid of her, they should at least help her to the front door. A couple of days later,

Mother was at the József Attila Neurological Clinic for a six-week sleeping cure.

At first, Grandmother hoped that a new job would restore her daughter's ability to climb stairs. She was glad when, having returned from her sleeping cure, Mother got another job. But the Bureau for Textile Exports, where Mother was employed as an assistant for eight hundred florints a month, was ignorant of the fact that its new errand lady could get no further than the lobby of whichever partner institution she was visiting. Then, if there was no elevator, she would stop, helplessly clutching her huge handbag to her bosom, the attaché cases containing the vital documents she had to deliver hanging from her arm.

The heads of the Bureau for Textile Exports quickly realised that to employ someone like Mother could pose a threat to the smooth running of their business. But they took into consideration their employee's social situation and the infinite goodwill that shone out of her, and when the next round of rationalisations came, they re-qualified her, making her a receptionist. But she was not on the regular payroll, and she received only half of her previous salary.

Mother had to pay for her agoraphobia with half her income, but she found the peace she was looking for in the draughty hall they called the reception room, where engineers and secretaries passed her by in quick succession. The secretaries would always greet her and perhaps even stop for a quick chat, and sometimes even the engineers paused by her desk. Then, taking the question 'How are you?' seriously, she'd give a detailed account of the present state of her health, at times with cheerful acceptance, and at other times, quietly weeping.

But her agoraphobia would not let up, even though they tried everything for it, not only the latest in psychotherapy, but even prayer. At the Brotherhood of Jews for Christ, Uncle Izidor Reiter led the prayers for her. 'Help our sister Erzsike,' he asked Jesus publicly, for he knew the remarkable ease with which the Redeemer had been known to solve even more complicated cases than this. 'Stand up and walk!' But these liberating words did not come. Where was the laying on of hands that could heal lepers? What was the use of dying on the cross when the sufferer was standing, even now, at the bottom of the stairs, facing the daily trial of her own Golgotha? This is what Robi Singer asked himself every time he passed the crucifix with the INRI* prescription on it gracing the prayer hall of the Brotherhood, and he fixed his gaze on Jesus, as if to hypnotise him, as if to make him speak. But, gentle as a lamb, his head bowed, the King of the Jews was busy with his own deadly stupor, and it seemed to Robi that he knew nothing of the agoraphobia of the errand lady demoted to the post of receptionist. No wonder, Robi Singer thought, when he was equally reluctant to make allowances for other horrors. Had Izidor Reiter heard what Robi was thinking, he'd have said, 'For I say unto you, redemption takes time, and there is no better medicine for what ails us on earth than patience.'

SOON AFTER Robi Singer's arrival, Gizike, the illiterate occasional maidservant, rang their bell. They had inherited Gizike from pre-war days when, as Grandmother said, they could afford to keep a maid. The open-hearted, industrious young woman was brought to their attention by a domestic agency and, ever since, she had been giving unrelenting testimony of her loyalty. When the family was forced to move into the ghetto, she bade them farewell amid tears, and as soon as they could return to their old apartment after the Liberation, she was there with her broom and rags to get rid of the traces of the Arrow Cross** family who had

---

* Latin, *abbrev. Iesvs Nazarenvs Rex Ivdaeorvm* (Jesus of Nazareth, King of the Jews).
** The Hungarian fascist party, led by Ferenc Szálasi, which played a significant role in the destruction of Hungarian Jewry in 1944.

occupied it. She hadn't left their side since, and practically considered herself their servant. She called Grandmother 'Your Ladyship' and Mother 'Little Ladyship', and Robi 'Young Gentleman'. Robi liked this sign of respect. We're someone special after all, he thought. Naturally, this would make Grandmother launch into a lengthy explanation of how they weren't gentlefolk, this set-up was just left over from the old times, and Gizike couldn't break the habit. On the other hand, Gizike knew that she could always count on Grandmother.

This time, for instance, she came because she wanted a hand with a petition to the council for temporary accommodation requesting a room and kitchen in place of the laundry room on the outskirts of town where she was now living. Petitions of this sort were always worded by Grandmother, who had a highly developed skill for jurisprudence. Besides, in Gizike's eyes, Grandmother was an oracle. The one weighty argument with which they hoped to soften the hearts of the authorities – even if to date they had nothing to show for it – was the fact that before the war Gizike's father had fought against the Romanians in the Red Army of the Hungarian Commune, for which he was later sent to a detention camp. Since her last petition the old man, whose interest in active politics was cooled for a lifetime by his camp experience, had quietly died in the cold and damp laundry room. 'And when I think, Your Ladyship,' Gizike said to Grandmother reproachfully, 'how dutifully I carried the bedpan for him.'

Grandmother said that the old man's death was neither here nor there as far as the merits of the case were concerned, for it was the living who needed a roof over their heads. Having said that, she took out Father's typewriter and in just half an hour wrote a petition that would have made any lawyer proud.

'Due to the sins of the accursed old regime I am illiterate,' she wrote in Gizike's name. She described in detail the heroism of the maid's father during the glorious times of the

Soviet Republic of Councils, and how with love and respect he kept his Red Army records under his pillow until the hour of his death.

When she heard the beautiful petition read to her, Gizike broke into profuse tears, declaring that she would now go and wax the floor of Little Ladyship's room. In the twinkling of an eye, she made for the hall to find the floor wax, which she always carried with her in one of her numerous bags; its odour floating around her, mingling with the smell of sweat and frozen garlic which she ate all the time.

'No, no,' Grandmother protested, 'the petition was a favour, but waxing the floor is work. You get paid for that.'

Grandmother didn't mind Gizike putting the apartment in order, but she didn't want her there when her daughter got back from the health centre. Last time Gizike made a *faux pas* as she was scrubbing the floor in Mother's room, saying, 'Your Little Ladyship Erzsike is so beautiful and your countenance is so fresh, how come you can't find yourself a man?'

On hearing this remark, the person it was aimed at stormed out to the kitchen and had a crying fit. As soon as her room was finished, she locked herself in and continued crying demonstratively. When she came out now and then for a drink of water, she looked at Gizike so reproachfully that you'd have thought she was blaming the girl for all the misfortune of her life.

'I won't be able to sleep again tonight,' she said to Grandmother, loud enough for the maid to hear.

Poor Gizike felt awful. She couldn't imagine how her innocent remark could have stirred up such a storm. In the end, she apologised, teary-eyed, to Erzsike, as Grandmother was gesturing to her, trying to tell her she should try a lot harder to keep quiet.

By that time they had stopped going to visit friends, and people avoided them, too. There was no knowing which innocent remark might upset Mother, who would compulsively start looking for the hidden insult, the intention to annihilate her. On the whole, these remarks passed the lips of friends and relatives quite innocently. They usually contained sound advice or encouragement, such as, 'Why don't you try sleeping without pills for a change?' or 'Why don't you ever go to the movies?'

But this would immediately get Mother's back up, and she would protest that no one's got the right to burst into her life – she doesn't burst into anybody else's life – and can take care of herself, thank you very much! But now that she was short on friends, she would hang on her mother's every word, lying in wait for any utterance that might jump-start the offence-taking mechanism. She lay in wait for the half sentences, most especially the comment that Grandmother used to make before she began trying to curb herself: 'Why don't you take better care of yourself?'

The illiterate Gizike could not understand this over-sensitivity and these easy tears, just as she could not have understood Dr Nádai's professional diagnosis. Gizike was as fit as a fiddle. She worked ten to twelve hours a day, and she took her poverty and solitude in her stride. She had been a servant since childhood, washing, ironing, cooking and cleaning for others, taking with her, as she went from house to house, the tart odour of sweat, the badge of her devoted labours.

In short, Grandmother did not want Gizike and Mother to meet. After she finally agreed to Gizike's waxing the floor, she began casting apprehensive glances at the clock, anxiously waiting for the moment when Mother would shout up from the street for someone to go downstairs and get her. But Mother did not shout upstairs. Instead, she made a sudden appearance at the door. She materialised there, then sneaked into her room – no mean feat, considering her size. Elated, and apparently having forgotten the last incident between them, she would tell Gizike the latest news. On her way home from Dr Nádai, she was just wondering who would help her upstairs, when she spotted Mr Román, the concierge, sweeping the street.

'Will you take me upstairs, Mr Román?' she asked.

The old man offered her his arm in response and said, with a sparkle in his eye, 'Erzsike, Little Ladyship, I'd gladly take you all the way to the registrar of marriages.'

Mother was so pleased with this sentence that she repeated it three times in succession, each time more happily and more loudly. Grandmother was not quite so happy when she heard about old man Román's courtship. He was over sixty, and a married man, so his offer was merely platonic. Still, she was glad to find her daughter in high spirits.

'I told you not to let yourself go,' she commended. 'Men still turn around to look at you when you pass by. Many a man would lick his fingers to have a wife like you.' At this point, Grandmother became alarmed, and for a moment she considered whether she might have said something her daughter could construe as an insult. But Mother was not to be tipped off balance. Gizike decided to heap praise upon praise.

'Erzsike, Little Ladyship, you're still as pretty as you were when you were forty-five,' she said. Then she asked, 'How old are you?'

And Little Ladyship Erzsike was more surprised than anyone by her own answer. 'I was just forty-two this summer, Gizike.'

They all had a hearty laugh over this. Grandmother laughed so hard that it brought tears to her eyes.

When the floors of both rooms were shining from the wax, they decided to make the occasion memorable with an ample dinner. This weekend Grandmother was nearly satisfied with the results of her shopping trip.

'Guess what?' she said proudly. 'I went to the Day and Night Supermarket. You can't imagine the choice. They had powdered egg, butter, cocoa, artificial lemon juice, black Russian bread, even two forint sausages. The line for apples was too long, but never mind, I'll get some tomorrow from the peasant at the Hunyadi Square market.'

This unexpected cornucopia of riches made the choice difficult, but Mother saved the day.

'Let's have pasta,' she proposed, 'and let's invite Gizike, too.'

At first the maid was reluctant, saying that the road to the laundry room in Pesterzsébet was long. First she had to take the Number 6 tram to Boráros Square, from where there was a bus, provided it went at all, and from the last stop she still had to walk about twenty minutes in the cold. In the end, when faced with the persistence of the family, she relented, and while the sound of the boiling pasta came from the kitchen stove, Grandmother went in search of the ingredients that would take the starchy pastry of uncertain consistency to a higher plane. Robi Singer accompanied her on her expedition in search of hidden reserves and in an obscure corner of the pantry, in a box with a Chicory Coffee label, he was elated to discover some stale ground walnuts, which Grandmother quickly combined with peach preserves she'd made the previous summer. And in just half an hour, there on the living room table, was the queen of all dishes: the layered pasta quickly put together and baked to a crispy brown in the oven. The poppy seeds, cottage cheese and vanilla sugar were missing, but it was still an evening to remember.

At first Robi Singer watched apprehensively, afraid there wouldn't be enough food left in the red enamel pot for his plate. Mother, too, who was sitting at the farther end of the table, cast anxious glances at the guest-sized portion that Grandmother piled on Gizike's plate. But soon they both saw that the ladle was dispensing the delicious food in generous amounts. A shame that Grandmother refused to eat. 'My gall bladder,' she said, and instead she drank tea with sweet biscuits.

After dinner, Mother took her medicines. Following

such an abundant meal, she began the ritual by taking two medicinal-charcoal pills, which, according to Grandmother, would counteract each other's effects. These were followed by a Belloid tranquilliser and a Nospa antispasmodic pill. Then Mother lay down on the divan so Grandmother could administer the eye-drops used to treat one of her more recent illnesses, the seventeenth – conjunctivitis. This part of the ritual was pointedly aimed at Gizike, too. Grandmother said, very tactfully, that God forbid, she should want to hurry Gizike away, but the buses on the outskirts of town were so unreliable.

Gizike took the hint. She thanked Grandmother for the dinner, for writing the petition and for the ten forints for the cleaning which, despite Gizike's protestations, Grandmother slipped into her pocket out in the hall. Even as she went down the stairs, Gizike was still blowing kisses to her hosts.

Then they locked and chained up the door, and all three went to bed. For a while, Robi Singer and Grandmother listened from the divan for signs of restlessness and sleeplessness from the other room, for it had become a habit with them. But this time Mother fell into a sound slumber, as if the peace and quiet that Dr Nádai had prescribed for her, and to which she therefore had a right, had at last settled on her troubled soul.

2

'YOU ALWAYS MAKE such a problem out of everything,'
Gábor Blum said to Robi Singer, shaking his head. They
were leaving the Vincze pastry shop on Flórián Square, and
their pockets were stuffed full of liquorice pieces, sweet
chocolate shavings, leftover bits of pound cake and layered
cake. They had winter ice-cream in their hands, whipped
cream that the old baker served in a cone.

'You always make such a problem out of everything,'
Gábor Blum repeated, studying his friend with his almond-
shaped eyes.

Gábor Blum was at least a head taller than Robi Singer.
His oval face, fleshy nose, creole skin and hair, which he
wore smoothed back, spoke of the mature man lurking
within the boy, the kind of handsome and self-confident
young man Robi Singer could never hope to be.

Gábor Blum's observation that Robi made a much bigger
deal of everything than he should have, was astute, to say
the least. Even wandering around the streets of Óbuda on
a late Monday morning, his pockets bulging with sweets,
a basically simple situation, was a real problem for him.
His grandmother regarded his pocket money – five forints,
which she dished out to him every Sunday evening – as
a right consecrated by custom, yet she never failed to
comment how sorely she would miss even this small sum,
especially towards the end of the month, when she'd always
be at a loss to pay the orphanage fees. Now, too, she said,
she'd have to go in person again, because if she mailed it in

she'd miss the deadline. She always made a point of telling her grandson to spend his pocket money sensibly, and if possible, to set some of it aside.

But every Monday at noon, after they left the state school, they headed straight for the Vincze pastry shop, where they made short shrift of the bulk of their weekly allowance, Robi Singer with sharp pangs of conscience, Gábor Blum with the greatest of ease. Every Monday Robi worried – could liquorice and winter ice-cream be considered sensible? But he always managed to convince himself that it could, seeing that the orphanage kitchen, which was half-staffed on Monday, served only caraway soup and semolina noodles – nothing like an ample lunch. Gábor Blum, on the other hand, didn't even try to excuse his extravagance, for he was firmly convinced that money was there to be spent.

His censorious head-shake from a moment ago, however, was not in response to Robi Singer's customary attack of bad conscience over the dispensation of his pocket money, but the question Robi had been posing as they walked from the state school in Kórház Street to the Vincze pastry shop on Flórián Square. Before he agreed to the circumcision Balla had suggested the previous Friday afternoon, shouldn't he tell his tutor that on Sunday mornings he accompanied his mother for prayers at the Jewish Brotherhood for Christ?

'Are you out of your mind?' Gábor Blum said. 'Balla's our tutor from Monday through Saturday, but what we do on Sunday, whether we go to a soccer game or Christian prayers, is none of his damn business.'

'It's not that simple,' Robi countered. 'Moses never said anything about soccer games, but he said not to worship foreign gods. For all I know, there might even be a law against circumcising anyone who has set foot in a Christian house of worship, even just once.'

'That's way over my head,' Gábor said. 'Why worry about a law that may not even exist? If Balla says get circumcised, get circumcised. I will, too, when he says so.'

Gábor Blum knew what he was talking about. He was the second of Balla's charges who was not circumcised when he should have been. Though he was two months Robi Singer's junior, he was approaching his own Bar Mitzvah, and there was no doubt that his tutor would soon be calling him to the teacher's room for a friendly chat. In fact, Gábor Blum was expecting it to happen any day now.

'What will you say to him?' Robi asked.

'What do you mean?' Gábor said, since the question had taken him by surprise.

'Will you agree to it?' Robi said.

'How can you ask a thing like that?' Gábor shot back, not believing his ears. 'Of course I will. And you will, too.'

'Still, it's a problem,' Robi pressed on.

'A problem, a problem,' Gábor Blum said, in imitation of his friend. 'What's so problematic about a small piece of skin?'

ALL THE JEWISH children's homes and live-in kindergartens that Robi Singer had been attending since the age of four had something in common. Besides a birth certificate and vaccination papers, they all required a document to prove that on the eighth day after his birth, Robi Singer had been duly circumcised. On these occasions, Robi's grandmother acted rather oddly. First she slowly and leisurely placed the documents on the table, then winced, the colour rising in her cheeks. You'd think she'd been caught on the tram trying to sneak a ride. Then she mumbled something about air raids and how terribly cold the winter of 5705 had been, and that, having come into the world prematurely, her grandson had been far too puny to undergo the procedure that Moses in his wisdom had made Law.

That first time, in the admissions office of the Zugliget children's home run by the Jewish World Congress, nobody questioned the reasons that Robi's grandmother gave for this omission. Obviously, nobody assumed that in some underhand manner she was trying to sneak a *goy* into a Jewish children's home. Still, they did warn her that by the time of Robi Singer's Bar Mitzvah, the omission would have to be remedied.

Up to this point, the story of Robi Singer's deferred circumcision bore a remarkable semblance to Gábor Blum's. Gábor Blum's mother had repeatedly left their apartment in Klauzál Street to get her newborn son circumcised, but something always came up. Sometimes the *briss** had to be put off because of air raids, while at other times the proverbially cold winter of the year 5705 forced her, too, to stay indoors. Eventually she forgot the solemn promise she had made to her husband before he was taken away to forced labour, never to return, that she would have their only child circumcised at the first opportunity.

The reasons given by the widow Mrs Blum were markedly similar to Robi Singer's grandmother's, except that Robi Singer's grandmother had a more judicious way of putting it. Since she felt no inclination to tell the whole story from beginning to end every time she was asked, she delicately referred to the circumstances that had impeded her grandson's *briss* as a *vis major*, or act of God. Gábor Blum's mother invariably put an end to the embarrassing subject with these words, 'When the time comes we'll do it,' and Grandmother merely kept bringing up the *vis major*.

Robi Singer's grandmother also said that around the time of her grandson's birth, not being circumcised may not have been such a calamity. The Arrow Cross were in the habit of dragging men under the archways of houses and

---

* The Covenant of Circumcision. It is the removal of the foreskin in order to make manifest 'the sign in the flesh' of the covenant made between God and Abraham. The ceremony of circumcision for every Jewish male child takes place on the eighth day after birth. If for medical (or other) reasons it cannot be carried out on the eighth day, then the circumcision may be postponed and is still valid if carried out later. But a boy born of a Jewish mother is automatically Jewish, whether or not he has been circumcised.

making them drop their pants to check whether they were Jews walking around without their yellow stars in violation of the law. When anyone was caught, he was promptly marched down to the Danube and shot into the icy river. Well, she had no intention of having her grandson caught with his pants down.

Strange as it may seem, Robi Singer's grandmother was convinced that the war was not over yet, and no logical argument could convince her otherwise. Admittedly, the Russians had beaten back the Germans, and at the last minute they'd frustrated plans for blowing up the ghetto. Still, things were not what they should be. For one thing, Germany had survived. For another, there were two Germanies now.

'One is supposed to be democratic,' she said, 'but we know what that means.' She wouldn't have been the least surprised if one morning she woke to the sound of air-raid sirens, and instead of going off to the Kerchief Dyers' Co-operative, she had to make for the nearest bomb shelter.

But Grandmother never said in so many words that she would rather die than let her grandson be circumcised. At least, not straight out. On the contrary, she kept reassuring Robi that it was nothing, 'just a little snip' that didn't take more than a minute. There would be a little pain afterwards, and he'd have forgotten all about it in a week. Besides, circumcision is healthy. It is even genteel.

'Just think,' she said. 'Every newborn male member of the British royal family – and that's some *mishpocheh*,* I can tell you – is made to participate in the joys of circumcision. You will be in the best company.'

Still, these attractive prospects did little to allay Robi Singer's trepidation at the idea of a white-frocked doctor approaching his naked lap with a knife. He'd stolen furtive glances at the other boys' genitals in the showers. They'd all had the operation, and they looked perfectly fine. Like

---

* Hebrew. Extended family.

Ambrus from the eighth grade, Robi Singer thought. He's bigger than any of us. The doctor who circumcised him was a true artist.

In Robi Singer's view, Ambrus had every reason to be proud of his big, long, majestic male organ, and he was. When the boys showered, he brandished his swelling tool at the others or lathered it lovingly. And there it was, at its peak, perched there like a crown, the dark brown glans.

'I'll never have one like that,' Robi Singer thought bitterly. Every time he pulled back his foreskin in the shower, he winced from pain. His sensitive glans protested against every drop of water hitting it, even the touch of his fingers. Yet wash you must, especially around the loins, as Balla never tired of telling them. 'Keep your whatchamacallits spotlessly clean,' he warned his students, adding with a mischievous smile, 'that's how the women like it.'

When Robi Singer studied his own manhood, he was invariably disappointed. His organ, he felt, was too short, even in the early-morning hours, when it stood erect. Wrinkled and colourless it fell limp against his unattractive scrotum, and when he pressed his two fleshy thighs together, the whole thingumajig disappeared, and when he looked in the long mirror by the bathroom door a figure without gender seemed to gaze back at him. If they snip anything off *this*, he tormented himself with self-irony, I'll never be able to strip in front of anyone else again. Gábor Blum can talk all he wants. He's got more than enough to give away.

But it was not just the idea of being foreshortened that bothered Robi Singer. There was something else lurking behind his fear. Again and again muddled dreams came to him, conjuring up the horror of his early childhood, the smell of ether and of carbonate, the rustle of the temperature charts, and the stealthy advance of white-gowned death through the wards of the hospital. He didn't even need the dreams. He just had to raise his left hand to his eyes to see his three maimed fingers, which had been joined by a thin, fin-like membrane at birth.

'Naturally, they will have to be separated,' the obstetrician had said. 'But don't you worry, it won't keep him from finding a wife.'

As a result of the bloody separation, three inflexible stumps graced Robi Singer's left hand. He was four years old at the time. Shaking her head, his grandmother said something about medical negligence, and then comforted Robi with the future prospect of some brilliant piece of plastic surgery that would put everything right. But Robi Singer had more than enough of the miracles of medical science. He had to put up with the other boys making fun of him and calling him 'goose-fingers', and he kept his left hand locked in a fist. A good thing it's not my right hand, he kept thinking.

Robi Singer worried that the doctor who would do the circumcision might also commit medical negligence, but this time on a part of his body of which there was only one, and not two, in case anything went wrong. What if the knife should slip and not stop at the foreskin? How will he show himself in front of the others in the showers? Will he find a wife? And is there plastic surgery to fix up damage of this sort? No wonder he was worried.

NATURALLY, Robi Singer had no intention of telling Balla about his participation in Christian services, something Gábor Blum talked about as easily as he would discuss a soccer game. No, he mustn't tell Balla, no matter what. It would pain him too much, and their intimate conversations about the history of the Jews would stop, and he was curious about so many things. He wanted to hear more stories and get good advice. Especially good advice.

For instance, he'd been meaning to ask Balla for the best protection against anti-Semitism. If someone should stop you in the courtyard of the state school and say, 'You're a Jew, aren't you?' what are you supposed to do? Or what should you do if the same thing happens on the street in Óbuda, when you come out of the yard of the synagogue? Clearly, anyone asking a thing like that already knows or suspects the answer. What is the proper way to act? Say yes, say no, demur, or make a run for it?

Gábor Blum, with whom he had discussed the subject in detail, believed in simple solutions. 'If a guy asked *me* a thing like that,' he said, 'I'd give him a once-over to see if he was stronger or weaker than me. If he was weaker, I'd ask what business it was of his, and if he insisted on being impertinent, I'd slug him. If he were stronger, I'd still ask what business it was of his, then break into a run.'

Robi Singer's point of departure was that he was weaker; besides, he was fat and couldn't run fast enough. Luckily, he hadn't met with any anti-Semites yet, and so the dilemma that he hoped to discuss with his tutor was purely theoretical. Besides, Balla had already provided a number of tips on how his charges should behave with non-Jews. In the state schools, for instance, they should receive good grades and show exemplary conduct, because, 'Whether we like it or not,' he said, 'people judge all Jews by how each of us behaves individually.' And then he added, 'We must know everything better than anyone else.'

In Robi Singer's experience, Balla's advice only served in a limited number of cases. It was plain to see that Mrs Oszwald, his Hungarian and history teacher at the state school, liked the students from the orphanage, because they were smart. If nobody volunteered to answer her questions, she turned to the dark-haired contingent in the class, put on an expectant smile and said, 'Well, my little Hebrews? How about you? I thought you always knew everything.' But not everyone in class liked this. A lot of people thought of the orphanage boys as eager beavers, especially the young hoodlums sitting in the back rows, who banded together into a close-knit group and called themselves the Bad Boys' Club.

Their leader was the lanky Oczel, the only Christian boy Robi Singer had managed to befriend. Actually, it was less of a friendship than a business and information set-up. Oczel gave Robi Singer stamps in exchange for postcards, inflation money for pictures of soccer players. Sometimes he offered Robi Singer paprika bacon, and on Passover Robi Singer ingratiated himself with crispy matzo. Robi Singer liked Oczel, possibly because he, too, was a half-orphan. His father had fallen at the Russian front without ever getting a chance to see his newborn son.

During recess, members of the Bad Boys' Club gathered together. They griped about their teachers and came up with all sorts of pranks against them. They pinched the chalk or the sponge and exploded paper water bombs in the halls. But they looked down on the good students even more than their teachers, and spent much of their time trying to figure out who from their class was squealing on them, informing the principal about their plans and conversations.

Even though he would have never dared to take part in their shenanigans, Robi Singer was highly impressed with the group. He was always lurking near them during recess, until one time Gábor Blum posed the following question: '*Must* you ingratiate yourself with those *goyim*?'* But the Bad Boys had no need of Robi Singer. As Oczel tactfully put it once, 'We've got nothing against you personally, except *you* tend to stick together, and so do *we*.' It was this 'you' and 'we' that preyed on Robi Singer's mind. It was a lot better than being called a dirty Jew on every street corner, but still. He wanted something more. He wanted to belong to the rest of the Hungarians, the people whose son he was by virtue of birth. On the face of it, the matter was simple enough. You had to mingle with them, live with them, feel their pain and sing their songs. But it wasn't!

Robi Singer felt profoundly Hungarian, sometimes to the

---

* The plural of 'goy'.

point of rapture. While Balla described the tragic events of the history of the Jews, Robi Singer would be thinking about the tragic fate of the Magyars. The Amalekites, the Medes and the Romans would invariably bring to mind the Turks and the Austrians. Once he'd read a story by Viktor Rákosi. It was called 'The Jewish Boy'. In the story, the youthful hero volunteers to join Kossuth's army. They're reluctant to take him because of his origins, but in the end he proves that, despite his alien religion, the heart that beats in his chest is a hundred per cent Magyar. However, it is too late by then and, as the sun sets over the blood-soaked battle field, and having shed profuse tears in honour of the little Jewish hero who fell fighting for the freedom of his country, the soldiers give him a magnificent funeral, and march on.

To Robi Singer's mind, the Hungarians had their fair share of suffering. They were not herded into a ghetto, *umberufen*,* and they were not dragged off to Auschwitz, *umberufen*, but they suffered just the same. In the history books, the description of every freedom fight, revolution or peasant uprising closed with a list of the reasons for its defeat. Mrs Oszwald was most insistent that her students memorize these reasons because, as she said, they were instructive about the future.

Poor Hungarians, Robi Singer thought, how they suffered before the Russians liberated them! Besides, they had more than just history to contend with. There was fate. Barely eighteen months before, in the month of *Tammuz* in the year 5714, the West German select soccer team beat the Hungarians three to two. School had not yet begun when this happened, but when the state school in Kórház Street opened its doors, all the students were still talking about the great calamity of the summer that had deprived Hungary of its position.

---

* Yiddish. Much used throughout Central Europe. It means 'God forbid', a deprecation to ward off evil. But in Hungary it is sometimes also used in the sense of 'to say the least'.

Robi Singer was never a soccer fan himself. Still, he felt that the events in Switzerland pointed beyond sports. He felt that what Oczel said was true, namely, that the Sports Minister was to blame, because he sold Hungary's honour for two hundred and fifty West German trucks. Someone had supposedly even seen the trucks drive along Stalin Road.

What a disgrace, Robi Singer thought, disgruntled, and concluded that, once again, the Hungarians were the victims of their fate. And to add insult to injury, it was the ancient enemy, Germany, who defeated them in front of the watchful eyes of the neutral, indifferent Swiss. He nearly cried with Szepesi, who broadcast the game over the radio, and the people on the street, too, who stood in line for the sports papers with uniformly mournful expressions.

Yes, Robi Singer thought, we must do all we can to be part of this nation. We must take it to our hearts and comfort it for its disastrous freedom fights, each one of which began with such high hopes, and for the soccer games, too, lost in their final moments. But how? That was the question. Oczel said that a Hungarian had only one brother, the Finn, and only one friend, the Pole. To Robi Singer's way of thinking, the Hungarians were very lucky, because the Jews didn't have any friends at all and were wandering around the world like orphans. There must be a way to bring Jews and Hungarians together, he thought. After all, they speak the same language and suffer the same fate.

A couple of years earlier, Robi Singer's grandmother had given him the following advice: 'If anybody asks about your origin, or which congregation you belong to, just tell them, "I am a Hungarian Jewish communist." You can't go wrong with that.'

Yes, Robi Singer thought, that's true as far as it goes. I am Hungarian. I was born and bred in Hungary. I am also a Jew. No one's ever said otherwise. As for being a communist, I am a communist because right after the liberation, Grandmother joined the Party. She pays her dues regularly and she visits District Headquarters out of gratitude for the Russians, because we have the Russians to thank for our lives.

Robi Singer liked this self-confident approach, and once when he went to Party headquarters with his grandmother, he stopped in front of Comrade Klein, the Party secretary, smiled, and repeated the adjectives he'd heard from his grandmother. On hearing the word 'Jew', Comrade Klein winced, however slightly, then gave Robi Singer some fatherly advice, that he might as well dispense with being a Jew; these days it was quite enough to be a communist. As for being Hungarian, well, that was only natural. On hearing this on their way home, Grandmother said that with a name like Klein, and especially with a *ponim** like Klein's, he really shouldn't talk against his own kind.

When Robi Singer told Oczel he was Hungarian, which was only natural, and a communist, too, but only out of gratitude, his friend was more diplomatic about dishing out the truth.

'Don't take it to heart,' he said tactfully, 'but it's not at all natural your being Hungarian.'

According to Oczel, who heard it from his mother, all communists were Jewish, while all Hungarians were Christians, so Jews couldn't be Christians. 'For one thing, they killed Jesus Christ.' This made Robi Singer's grandmother highly indignant. 'What do you *mean* Jews can't be Christians?' she said. 'Jesus Christ was Jewish, too.' Then, after a short pause, she added that the Redeemer was also the first communist.

Robi Singer's mother had found a job at the Bureau for Textile Exports by then, where she soon befriended Anna Marie, a slender, blonde draughtswoman. Whenever she got the chance, Anna Marie would join Robi Singer's mother at her post after work, and they would pray together, including

---

* Hebrew, *colloq.* 'Face', in Hungarian, means a 'fellow'.

Grandmother and Robi Singer in their prayers. Anna Marie was humility incarnate. She even talked about the weather with piety. 'What blessed weather we had yesterday!' She referred to Jesus Christ only as 'He'. She suffered the vicissitudes of life with eager Calvinist zeal, including the greatest calamity of all, the fact that her husband had spent years in prison because he taught religion on the sly.

Robi Singer tried to ingratiate himself with Anna Marie by telling her that though he was Jewish, he was really a communist out of gratitude to Jesus Christ, who was also a communist. What he meant to say, in short, was that he, Robi Singer, was really a Christian.

'Don't be silly, my dear,' the draughtswoman said with a smile, stroking Robi Singer's head. 'You can't be a Christian and a communist at the same time – the prisoner and the prison warden. We Christians forgive the communists just as He forgave those who tortured him. But have you ever heard of a communist forgiving anyone at all? No, son, you're not a communist, for it is written all over you that you are looking for Him, and if you are looking for Him, you shall find Him.' And with that, she kissed Robi Singer's forehead.

If this goes on much longer, Robi Singer thought, I'll go stark, raving mad.

To Robi Singer's mind, Comrade Klein's reasoning seemed the least convincing of all. Even the facts contradicted Comrade Klein. After all, one is a Jew by virtue of birth, but a communist by virtue of choice. Also, why didn't Comrade Klein ever talk about Christ around his Party district if – as his grandmother said – Christ was a communist, and therefore a comrade? And while we're on the subject, why doesn't Grandmother ever talk about Christ being killed? It's no secret. Oczel says so, and look at all those crucifixes that remind you of it everywhere. And also, why doesn't Oczel come clean and say that the Jews who killed him, if indeed it was the Jews, killed one of their own?

Anna Marie seemed the most reasonable. Anna Marie said that in that ancient story in Jerusalem, the Jews were not entirely without blame because when Pontius Pilate asked the multitude who they wanted crucified, they all said, the man from Nazareth. 'But He forgave them,' Anna Marie added, 'and He asked the same of His Father, and He asks the same thing of us. We must always forgive, regardless of the circumstances.'

This demonstration of unbounded love had a profound effect on Robi Singer. After all, if it were that simple, what could Jews and Christians, Hungarians and communists possibly have against each other? Carefully embedding this in a discussion about history, Robi asked Balla whether he also felt that the idea was commmendable.

'Commendable, yes,' Balla said with a sad shake of his head. 'But just look what they're doing. They've been persecuting the Jews by fire and sword for two thousand years because of this man, whom they consider their Redeemer, and who they themselves say was Jewish. Is this what you call the religion of love? They've loved us with burning stakes, and they've loved us with pogroms. They've loved us with concentration camps, and they've loved us with gas chambers. Well, I want none of their love.' Balla gave a short, bitter laugh. 'And I want none of their forgiveness either. Let them forgive themselves, if they can.'

ROBI SINGER DECIDED that Balla was too hard on Christians. What's past is past. Besides, they can't all be blamed. There was definitely something in what Christ said on the cross. People don't always know what they're doing. Anna Marie, for instance. She certainly meant well when she took Robi Singer along with her to the Catholic festival at Fót one Sunday morning in summer. They went by bus, and the weather was lovely. 'You will see a real service, Robi dear,' Anna Marie promised, for she considered everything that occurred at the prayer house of the Jewish Brotherhood a pale imitation of Christianity. Indeed, the psalms under the huge roof rang out more fully and the preaching had more conviction to it, and the elderly preacher did not go from pew to pew, making the faithful stand up and declare their faith. He must have considered his brethren as finished Christians, it seems, even though he roundly chastised them for unspecified sins, demanding that they repent.

Such honesty impressed Robi Singer, but nothing impressed him as much as the fact that, despite such censorious words, none of the faithful got up in a huff and left.

Anna Marie and he exchanged a look. 'Isn't it beautiful,' Anna Marie whispered.

'Yes,' Robi whispered back with a seraphic smile on his lips as he slipped his hand into Anna Marie's own.

After the service, Anna Marie led Robi Singer over to a group of boys who were standing around in front of the church.

'I must go to a seminar now,' she said. 'You go with them to Sunday School.' And before Robi Singer could protest, Anna Marie disappeared among the churchyard trees.

That wasn't very nice of her, Robi thought with a sense of foreboding.

The old preacher took the boys to a church annex, where they were seated in a small, sparsely furnished room, facing a crucifix hanging on the wall. The chairs were placed in the round, with the preacher in the middle. There was a table with bibles and psalm books on it. While they were singing, Robi Singer moved his lips mutely, but when they started the Lord's Prayer, he joined in because he knew it by heart from the Jewish Brotherhood. Next, the preacher started to ask the boys about stories from the Bible, ones Robi had never heard of, and he panicked. The preacher was going around the room with questions, and his turn was about to come.

Robi Singer cursed himself for letting Anna Marie leave

him behind in Sunday School. This was far worse than the Monday School, or state school, where only his shortcomings in maths or geography could be exposed. Here he would be exposed for what he was, ignorant and different from the rest – a stranger.

He barely had time to reflect on this calamity, when the old preacher turned to him and said, 'How did the Lord Christ distribute the bread among the multitude?'

Equally! Robi Singer wanted to say. But he realised that this could hardly be the right answer. He felt the colour rising in his cheeks, and his knees began to shake, as they sometimes did in state school. But instead of his usual answer, 'I didn't do my homework,' he said, almost inaudibly, 'I am not Catholic.'

The others stared at him without fully understanding.

Not so the old preacher. 'In that case,' he said softly, 'what might you be, son?'

'I mean, sir,' Robi Singer stuttered, 'what I mean to say, sir... I mean, I'm not a Catholic yet, sir. For the time being, I am still a Jew.'

Robi Singer stretched out the sentence on purpose, hoping that he could avoid having to say the word 'Jew'. It was taboo. He found himself hating every letter of it. And being his only introduction in this barren room, it was tantamount to the most profound humiliation. The moment it passed his lips, he felt an invisible but impregnable wall rising between himself and the others.

In the strained silence, one of the boys started giggling. That put the others at ease, and before long the whole Sunday School was laughing in chorus. To alleviate the embarrassment of his exposure, Robi Singer laughed with them. Only the preacher's face remained grave. In fact, it looked more and more grave by the minute.

'What's so funny?' he said, his anger rising. 'Aren't you ashamed of yourselves? The Jews are just like us.' Then he turned to Robi Singer. 'Sit down, son,' he ordered, and put the question about the bread to someone else to answer in class.

'THERE YOU GO AGAIN, making a problem out of everything,' Gábor Blum said when Robi Singer told him of his doubts about Jesus Christ. 'After two thousand years *you* want to figure out who killed him? Even Dönci the "Sheriff" wouldn't know the answer to that one.'

Gábor Blum was of the opinion that Magyar, Jew, Christian and communist had nothing in common, and that people shouldn't try to be too many things at once. It was asking for trouble.

'Let's stick to being Jews,' he said, 'that won't cost us.' Then he shook his head. 'People say we should thank the Russians for our lives. Sure. But just look at the map. Their real destination was Berlin, and we happened to be in the way. They *had* to liberate us. Besides, the commies aren't perfect either. They take everything away from you, your shop, your house, even the hospitals. And don't forget,' – and at this point his expression darkened – 'they evicted us from Queen Wilhelmina Avenue.'

THE LOVELY tree-lined boulevard where the old orphanage building stood originally bore the name of the Dutch Queen Wilhelmina, but it was later re-christened in honour of the Russian writer Gorky. Nobody raised an eyebrow, because by then Theresa Boulevard had long since been re-christened Lenin Boulevard, Customs House Boulevard had become Tolbuchin Boulevard, and it was only due to blind luck that Klauzál Street, where Gábor Blum's mother waited for him to come home at the weekends, had escaped the general carnage.

All this happened a long time ago. In the month of *Tishri*, in the year 5713, during Bible class, Balla was telling his charges about the exodus from Egypt, when he stopped and announced, 'By the way, we will have our own exodus soon.' There was enormous excitement all around, but in response to his charges' questions, Balla would only say that a certain authority insisted that they move out of the beautiful three-storey villa in City Park, near the Israeli Embassy, which had given shelter to the male orphans and half-orphans of the Jewish community for more than half a century.

Gábor Blum said there was no authority behind the eviction, it was the commies who wanted to get the Jewish orphans out of there because they'd set their sights on the beautiful villa for themselves. In biblical times, the Pharaoh used every means at his disposal to keep Moses and his people in their place, and it took the Lord's intervention and the Ten Plagues to make him change his mind. Not so *this* particular authority. This particular authority was pressing for an exodus, and now it was the Jews who, contrary to custom, wanted to stay put.

It was rumoured that when they heard the news around Yom Kippur, the Board of Trustees held a meeting and someone suggested that they write a letter to the leader of the nation* who, as luck would have it, was *unsereiner*, a Jew. With reference to this happy circumstance, the speaker reasoned, they could apply for exemption from the threat of eviction. Except – or so the story went – upon hearing this, a rabbi, who apparently had nothing more to lose, threw up his hands saying: '*Seid ihr Meschugge?*** Isn't it bad enough that the scoundrel is one of us? Must we *remind* him of it?' And so the idea of writing the petition was dropped.

As far as Robi Singer was concerned, the decision of his highly esteemed superiors was tantamount to a sin of omission. The leader of the nation was a wise and kind-

---

* Refers to Mátyás Rákosi, First Secretary of the Hungarian Communist Party, the 'all-powerful' leader of Hungary from 1949-1953. He enjoyed a personality cult in Hungary similar to that of Stalin in the Soviet Union.
** Yiddish. 'Are you mad?'

hearted man, even the *goyim* knew that. At the state school their teachers kept saying that he was their Wise Leader and the Father of All Children. Robi Singer felt that this would have been his chance to prove it. But it was no use crying over spilt milk. The Jews had taken so many things in their stride, one more wasn't going to make much of a difference.

And so, the sad day finally came in the month of *Shevat* in the year 5714, when the Boys' Orphanage of Pest had to relocate to Óbuda. At least the Lord didn't have to bother separating the waters of the Danube for, accompanied by their tutors, the hundred and ten boys crossed Margaret Bridge on the Number 66 tram. Also, the wandering in the wilderness didn't last anywhere near forty years, just forty minutes, provided you're willing to consider Frankel Leó Street and Lajos Street a wilderness. On the other hand, the empty Zichy Street apartment house at their journey's end didn't resemble the Promised Land by any stretch of the imagination.

Rabbi Schossberger himself acknowledged the glaring difference. 'From now on,' he announced during their first prayers in their new home, 'we will have to make do with less. But considering what our people went through during the past 5700 years, we mustn't gripe. After all, it's a miracle that we're still around at all.'

On hearing these words of comfort, Robi Singer concluded that miracles were nothing special, because a miracle is the state of things at any one time, and so it is a miracle simply by virtue of being. Until that moment, the magnificent building on Queen Wilhelmina Avenue had been a miracle, and from now on the decrepit apartment house in Zichy Street would be a miracle, too. But it was no miracle when, having run out of funds, the orphanage was forced to sell its holiday home on the shores of the Danube – a haven where every year, in the month of *Sivan* or *Tammuz*, the boys would go via the Petőfi or Kossuth steamers to spend the summer. From now on, they were told, they would have to be content with a smaller miracle – their daily walk over Stalin Bridge to visit the People's Baths.

They hoped to never experience a worse exchange! The roads of City Park were full of elegant automobiles, while in Óbuda they were lucky to have the Number 33 tram clatter past. In Queen Wilhelmina Avenue they'd had their own yard, while now they had to make do with the back yard of the synagogue where they'd march in an orderly file from their new lodgings. And where was the spacious dining hall with the kitchen and pantry behind it? Where the modern showers, the central heating? Where the large salon which on holidays could be turned into a synagogue by opening the concertina doors? And what did they have now? Damp walls and cramped rooms, iron stoves that had to be fired up every morning, cramped bathrooms with rusty shower heads that wouldn't let you adjust the water temperature properly. In short, anything and everything was incomparably shabbier than in Pest.

But it was the organ that pained Robi Singer's heart the most. It had been a majestic instrument through which the Lord himself seemed to speak to them, especially on the high holidays, when Mr Lisznyai conducted the orphanage choir.

On that fateful day towards the end of the month of *Tevet* when the boys were at their farewell lunch in the building on Queen Wilhelmina Avenue, Aunt Francisca, the tutor of the younger boys, suffered a nervous breakdown, whilst Balla paced up and down with a sombre expression on his face and the oil print of Moses Mendelssohn rolled up under his arm. For his part, Robi Singer headed upstairs to the salon. The tables and chairs were gone, and only the white lines on the dusty floor marked where the furniture had been. But the solitary organ pipes were still standing somewhere up high. If only they could sing the praises of the Lord one last time, Robi Singer thought, before they end up in the hands of that certain nameless authority, or some other *goyim*. Later, as he headed for Óbuda on the Number 66 tram with his meagre belongings hanging from his shoulder, Robi felt a sense of indignation. They had committed a sin, he felt, when they left the organ, the Almighty's musical instrument, behind the Red Sea.

STILL, BEING JEWISH has its advantages, Robi Singer thought, even in Óbuda. He felt a surge of joy, for instance, whenever the Torah curtain was drawn back in the Óbuda synagogue and the back-cloth was revealed like a firmament of stars far brighter than anything in real life. And when the *Shabbes* candles were lit on Friday night and they said *broche** around the long dining table, eager for their humble but festive supper. Or when on the first night of Pesach they set a place for the Prophet Elijah, calling him to join them with a song – that too was beautiful. '*Elijahu hanavi*,' they sang year after year. The guest they would have liked to join them never showed up, but Robi Singer would always glance at the empty place-setting with anticipation, and at the open door and window, too, for there was no telling where a prophet might choose to appear. Robi also loved it when a Bar Mitzvah boy shared the small presents he received from the congregation with his peers, like the thirty Pioneer chocolate bars that the fully orphaned Fried from the eighth grade handed around the previous year. He, Robi Singer, would do likewise once he was initiated as a Son of the Commandments. He would be liberal with his presents, if only out of gratitude for having survived the ordeal of circumcision.

Of course, the boundless joys of orphanage life were as nothing compared to *Eretz Yisroel*, of which Balla told them many a story. For instance, Balla had told them that

---

* From the Hebrew '*bracha*'. A blessing, a prayer of thanksgiving and praise, said especially at meals.

in the Promised Land the boundaries between 'mine' and 'yours' were nonexistent, joy and sorrow were shared by all, and the eternal sunshine that ripened the fruit shone on everyone in equal measure. In that ideal community, even the most ill-humoured Jew changed his ways, if only he felt like it.

Thanks to Balla's accounts, Robi Singer imagined *Eretz Yisroel* as one big, happy orphanage, though he secretly hoped that there was somewhere to go to at the weekends, even there. The trouble was that nobody knew when they would finally reach the Promised Land. Around the New Year, in the month of *Tishrei*, Jews solemnly promised each other that next year they would meet in Jerusalem, but this seemed as hopeless as a visit from the Prophet Elijah, who refused to appear despite their persistent invitations. 'Patience,' Balla said, 'patience. What's the rush?'

AFTER LIGHTS OUT in the dormitory, where their beds stood side by side, *Eretz Yisroel* was a frequent topic of conversation between Robi Singer and Gábor Blum. Since he and his mother had been considering emigration for years, Gábor Blum counted as something of an expert on the subject. Gábor Blum's mother's brother lived in Tel Aviv, where he went straight from a camp after the war. Now, after many years, they'd finally had a letter from him. He was running a small haberdashery shop. He was not rich, but he could provide amply for his family. 'We should leave, too,' Gábor Blum's mother kept saying, until the frontiers were closed and it was too late. She had no one left in Hungary, she said. Besides, she was a sales assistant at the Fashion Palace, and you could be a sales assistant anywhere.

For years she walked past the Israeli Embassy on Queen Wilhelmina Avenue with her eyes averted, not daring to go inside to ask for a visa. Lately, however, a friend told her confidentially that the Hungarian authorities had become more permissive. You didn't have to fear retaliation any more if you applied for an emigration visa. The situation, indeed, must have improved, and the letter Gábor Blum and his mother received from Tel Aviv at long last seemed to prove that. 'Anyway,' whispered Gábor Blum excitedly from the adjacent bed, 'we're off to Tel Aviv.'

Robi Singer thought longingly of *Eretz Yisroel* himself, but he suspected that his path to the Promised Land would be a lot more tortuous than his friend's. For instance, would his grandmother undertake such a strenuous journey at her age, not to mention his mother, who couldn't even climb the stairs without help? How would she manage to board an ocean liner? And would *Eretz Yisroel* admit a Jew who had become a believer in Christ?

All the same, Robi Singer imagined the beautiful letters he would write to his mother from sunny Tel Aviv. He would even send her packages through Ikka.* He listened as though enchanted to Gábor Blum's accounts of Tel Aviv, Herzl Avenue and his uncle's haberdashery shop – which in Gábor's mind had been transformed into a veritable Fashion Palace. Then there were the eternally blue skies, the figs and oranges, and the long-awaited moment when he, Gábor Blum, would proudly show the Israeli border guards the document proving that he had been circumcised, thereby clearing the last barrier to the land of his ancestors. He felt as if he were already walking the streets of Tel Aviv, Jerusalem and Haifa, and he was pleased to share this imagined happiness with his friend Robi Singer. There was just one question preying on their minds – would the Promised Land have a pastry shop as good as the one on Flórián Square?

---

* A Hungarian government bureau of the 1950s. Its main task was to check every single parcel sent from non-communist countries to Hungarian citizens and to make sure that no anti-communist propaganda material could pass through.

THEY REACHED the corner of Mókus Street and Zichy Street deep in thought, silently licking the sweet whipped cream. They had just rounded the corner when Gábor Blum gave Robi a nudge. 'Look! There's your grandmother!'

At first, Robi Singer thought his friend was pulling his leg. But then he spotted his grandmother coming through the orphanage gate and heading for the suburban train station by the Danube with short, quick steps. Robi's feet were rooted to the ground. What was Grandmother doing there? And why didn't she wait for him? His first impulse was to shout after her, but she seemed to be in a greater hurry than usual.

Then Robi realised why Grandmother had visited the orphanage. The monthly dues. She must have come into some money in the morning, and in order not to miss the deadline, she had gone personally to the orphanage's cashier with the 220 forints. Robi Singer remembered the first time he'd seen Grandmother hurry off in such haste. He was four years old when she took him by the hand one day and led him to a children's home in the Buda hills. 'I must go and attend to something,' she had said to Robi. 'Wait for me right here.'

Robi Singer had waited in the garden, its trees practically hiding the building from view. He waited patiently until he spotted Grandmother, who was already outside the iron gate by then, trying to sneak unseen to the bus stop. That was when Robi realised that what Grandmother had had to attend to was him. She wanted to avoid having to say goodbye, so she'd sneaked out the back way. But why was she sneaking away from him now?

'No,' Robi said with sudden resolve. 'That's not Grandmother. Just somebody who looks like her.'

'YOUR ESTEEMED GRANDMOTHER said you're afraid of being circumcised,' Balla announced in the duty officer's room that afternoon. 'But I told her that to the best of my knowledge you're a brave lad whose hero is Bar Kochba. I know that at times even the brave are afraid. Still, I am hurt, just a bit, that you never mentioned your fear to me. Your esteemed grandmother also said that circumcision is a mere formality, and of course, she's quite right. She's a wise woman, *alle Achtung*,* my hat off to her. But the Lord likes formalities, and He had His reasons for marking His people. On the one hand, circumcision is a mere trifle. On the other hand, what kind of a Jew is it who won't agree to such a trifle as a testimony of his faith? You won't disappoint me, son, will you?'

After this portentous preamble, Balla offered Robi Singer some candy, then went on talking as if he were continuing their accustomed discussions of history.

'Look, son,' he said, 'you are what you were born to be, there's no getting around that. Many are leaving the faith, especially in these difficult times. They convert. They become renegades. They do their best to be regarded as Christians. They live as Christians, and they think as Christians. But all in vain. Their own kind disown them, while strangers won't accept them among themselves. And what happens? For the rest of their lives they're ashamed of the thing they should be proud of, and are proud of the thing they should be ashamed of. The mark on their bodies, which they received as an honour, becomes a badge of shame. Let me give you an example,' Balla continued, switching to the manner he used when discussing history. 'In the last century, there lived a German Jewish poet. His name was Heinrich Heine. Don't worry if you haven't heard of him. They don't teach his work in school, and I haven't talked about him either. Anyway, when he was young, this Heine converted and became a Lutheran, a blameful thing, to be sure. But

---

* German. 'Attention all.'

Heine was a great poet and a wise man. Nothing shows his wisdom better than the sad comment he once made about his own circumcision, namely, that although he converted, what was once snipped off would never grow back again. Yes,' Balla said in summation, 'the *briss* is forever. It is our irrevocable covenant with God. Besides, it wasn't just a whim with Him. The *briss* is hygienic. It didn't kill Heine, and it's not going to kill you. Understand?'

Robi Singer wanted to say something, but he couldn't get a word out. He sucked on the candy, throwing pleading glances at Moses Mendelssohn, as if asking him for advice. Balla sympathised with his charge's confusion, and he went on to reassure him.

'You needn't answer right now, son,' he said. 'But think about it, because it's more pressing than I thought. I wouldn't rush you myself. It's the rabbinate. And now, you may go.'

As Robi Singer got up from the ottoman, he had butterflies in his stomach. He nodded respectfully, then made for the door. His hand had just touched the door knob when Balla, who seemed to be immersed in a book, called after him. 'Wait, son!' Robi Singer turned around, terrified. 'Tell your friend Blum I want to see him as well.'

MR WEISZ, the tutor on night duty that day, was short, red-haired and a strict disciplinarian. He didn't like sending boys home for the weekend indiscriminately, because in his view the visits had a damaging effect on group discipline. He also felt that Balla's method of instruction was far too lenient. He was right to the extent that Balla couldn't have handled his own seventh and eight graders. They were the ones making the most racket just now, as they waited for dinner, so that Weisz had to make them say *broche** three times before it could be heard. Meanwhile, the steaming

---

* From the Hebrew '*bracha*'. A blessing, a prayer of thanksgiving and praise, especially at meals.

cauliflower soup was on the table. And when the din would not let up, Weisz made each of his charges repeat his favourite saying, 'Order is Heaven's first Law,' three times, but that didn't help either. At that point he lost his patience and roared that if there was so much as a peep out of anyone during dinner, they'd curse the day they were born. That seemed to have done the trick, and a profound silence ensued.

Certainly, Robi Singer had no intention of giving Weisz an excuse for making good his promise. He wouldn't have made any noise, anyway, because he was getting increasingly worried. Why was the chair next to him still empty? What was keeping Gábor? What could his friend and Balla be talking about?

The trouble started when the soup tureen reached him, by which time it had to be tipped on its side to fill the ladle with soup. Fried tried to help from the other end of the table, but he must have tipped it too much, because the tureen rolled on its side and its contents trickled toward Robi Singer's plate, with some cauliflower florettes swimming in the makeshift stream. As Robi tried to steady the tureen, he brushed the ladle off the table. It was made of heavy metal, and it landed on the stone floor with a resounding clang. Whatever soup the far from spotless tablecloth had not absorbed dripped leisurely after it.

Weisz, who had just sat down at the head of the table in anticipation of his dinner, was now forced to interrupt his meal when, having found a new object and direction for itself, the bubble of deep silence burst into life once again. The boys ran across from the nearby tables and stood around the ladle lying on the stone floor like people standing around the victim of an accident on the street. 'It was Robi Singer,' one of the boys shouted, and this was immediately echoed by a whole choir of boys, 'It was Singer! It was Singer!' Embarrassed, Robi bent down to pick up the ladle, a clear admission of his guilt. By the time he realised what he was doing, Weisz was by his side, standing over him with his feet planted apart, a colossus. He came so close that their bodies almost met. Then he began screaming at the top of his voice. 'People slaved over this soup. There is blood, sweat and tears in this soup. And if you don't appreciate that, you're a scoundrel, and I don't care how well you read Hebrew.'

The meaning of Weisz's words reached Robi Singer's consciousness some time after they'd split his ear drums, but when they hit him, he couldn't help but think that if there was work in the soup, it did not matter more than the wasted cauliflower florettes. Though he felt like laughing, he managed to restrain himself, yet a hint of a smile appeared in the corner of his lips. 'What's so funny? What's so funny about other people working their fingers to the bone? Well, you won't find it amusing for long, I promise you!'

He grabbed Robi Singer and began shaking him. He could not bring himself to make good his promise of a thrashing, though, and this only infuriated him further. In the meantime, he never once stopped singing accolades to the nobility of work well done.

At this point, though, Robi Singer was no longer listening to Weisz's words, nor did he mind being shaken out of his pants. First the reddening shame disappeared, then he lost his patience. Let's get it over with, he thought, even a slap in the face is a whole lot better than this unbearable screaming, so when Weisz stopped to catch his breath, in the shocked, profound silence, Robi screamed back at him. 'Stop shouting at me, you arsehole, I'm not deaf!'

His words frightened him. It can't be, he couldn't have said this. Students with much more pluck than him, like Ambrus in the eighth grade, maybe even they wouldn't be caught being so brazen and impudent. Calling a teacher an arsehole and shouting at him as if they were equals, that's asking for trouble. It was heroism in the face of death. And in the mind's eye he could see Bar Kochba dressed to the hilt in knightly armour, his eyes defiant, readying himself for the decisive battle. You could never have humiliated the Son of the Star about some stupid spilt cauliflower soup. And instantly, Robi Singer felt – could almost hear, in fact – the thrill of victory coursing through his veins. This must be the happiness one reads about in books, he reflected.

Weisz's arms, which a moment ago were still shaking him, were now hanging limp. His eyes were clouded by incomprehension and bewilderment, and for a long moment he seemed incapable of speech. 'You haven't heard the last of this,' he said, almost inaudibly, and walked back to the head of the table and resumed his seat.

Just then, Balla entered the dining room with Gábor Blum trailing behind, wearing a serene, otherworldly expression on his face. He'd come to make excuses for his charge being late, Balla explained.

Taking advantage of the situation, Weisz turned to him. 'I'm glad you're here,' he said with open sarcasm. 'One of your boys needs to be taught his manners.' Then he turned to Robi Singer. 'Come here, son, and repeat what you just said to me.'

In the twinkling of an eye, Balla was on top of the situation. Before Robi Singer could get a word out, he tactfully steered Weisz away from the table and whispered something in his ear. They had their backs to the boys, who were waiting with bated breath to see what was brewing. Then Weisz turned around, his smile of satisfaction and anticipation revealing that he was about to return the insult to his person with interest, what's more, without having to resort to violence. He walked to the head of the long dining table so he could be seen and heard by everyone. Then, his voice ringing out clear and strong as a trumpet, he said, 'What's this I hear? Our little favourite isn't even circumcised? Where's the knife? Someone hand me a knife!'

*

'Did he really not offer you candy?' Robi Singer asked Gábor in the middle of the night.

'I already told you,' his friend said in a whisper, 'I'm sleepy.'

'And he didn't mention Heine either?'

'Who is Heine?' Gábor asked with annoyance from the adjoining bed.

'Well, what did he say then?' Robi Singer continued plying his friend with questions. 'What reason did he give you? Why do you need to get circumcised?'

'For the same reason you do,' Gábor said. Then he started giggling. 'And also because women like it better with a rim. Now go to sleep!'

3

POOR Uncle Móric passed away. It was a real calamity, even though poor Uncle Móric never existed in the first place. That is to say, he existed, all right, but if Grandmother ever got wind of it, all hell would break loose.

This was the sad, problematic state of affairs that confronted Robi Singer when he came home on Saturday afternoon. Grandmother, who was out in the kitchen washing the dishes, looked concerned as she turned to him. 'There's something terribly wrong with your mother,' she said, 'Go. Maybe she'll tell *you* what it is.'

Robi's mother was lying on her bed, which took up half the room. She was fully clothed, her eyes were red from crying, and she kept blowing her nose and dabbing at her eyes with the half-dozen or so handkerchiefs that lay scattered on the duvet. Her lips quivered when she spoke Uncle Móric's name, and told Robi how she found out about his death. As she was speaking, Robi felt terrorstruck. *Sh'ma Yisroel!*[*] How will they ever keep the reason for this show of grief from Grandmother? How will they keep from her the fact that the widow Mrs Andor Singer had now become, in a manner of speaking, widowed for the second time?

Uncle Móric's full name was Mór Hafner. He was a gentleman's tailor by profession, now an employee of the

---

[*] The first two words of the central Jewish prayer, 'Hear, O Israel: The Lord is our God, the Lord is one!' which is said twice daily and consists of three paragraphs from the Bible. It is also used colloquially by Hungarian Jews on hearing news that is shocking or startling.

Forge Ahead Co-operative and Mother's boyfriend. That word, though, never passed Mother's lips. Even on the rare occasion that she called Uncle Móric her 'friend', a blush rose to her cheeks.

Mór Hafner had entered their lives two years previously, when he'd sent a courteous postcard asking Robi Singer's mother to meet him at the Café Terminal on Saturday afternoon the following week. 'The fact is,' he wrote, 'I need some urgent typing, and Mrs Komlós, your former colleague, was kind enough to give me your address as a first-rate typist. Kindly come to the Café Terminal at four in the afternoon. I will be holding a *New Life*[*] in my hand for the purpose of identification.'

Mother was pleased that after so many years of being a simple receptionist, someone still remembered her at her former place of employment and thought of her as a first-class typist. There were other signs, besides, that Mother took special note of the stranger's invitation.

When Robi Singer came home from the orphanage that hot summer's afternoon, he found his mother in front of the large wardrobe, going through her things. What was a first-rate typist supposed to wear for an important business interview? The pale yellow suit, which was such a sensation at the last Bureau for Textile Exports company outing that the director was heard to say, 'Our colleague Mrs Singer is one of the best dressed members of the assistant staff?' Or, considering the pleasant sunshine, should she wear the white dress with red butterflies that Grandmother had made for her walks on Margaret Island? No, the red butterfly dress was too loud, the stranger might think she had designs on him.

Grandmother watched her daughter's careful preparations with satisfaction. She was glad that her daughter had had her hair permed that morning, and that she took such pains

---

[*] A weekly Hungarian Jewish newspaper that has been publishing in Budapest for over fifty years.

getting dressed for her meeting. 'You see,' she said by way of encouragement, 'I always said that at the age of forty you're too young to neglect yourself.'

Once a year, Grandmother altered the two beautiful outfits, the pale yellow suit and the frock with the red butterflies, on her sewing machine, depending on whether her daughter had lost or gained weight since the summer before. But this time around, the yellow suit proved too tight, and for some unfathomable reason the red butterfly frock was much too loose. There was no time for Grandmother to let anything out or to take anything in. Since the yellow suit ripped at the seams in two places when Mother tried it on, they decided in favour of the red butterfly dress. Grandmother suggested that Mother put on the gold-plated silver necklace her older sister, poor Aunt Jutka, had given her before the war but which, out of respect for the dead, she never wore. On the other hand, this solitary representative of the family store of jewels sported a black 'Nefertiti head' design, just the thing to counterbalance the brightness of the red butterfly frock. Let the stranger see that he's dealing with a decent woman who doesn't care to flirt. Mother's dark brown orthopaedic shoes didn't go well with the red butterflies, so she took out the other pair, which she hardly ever wore. They were not very comfortable, but at least they were red.

As a last step, Robi Singer's mother applied a generous amount of powder to her face and darkened her eyebrows with the head of a match. Standing in front of the big hall mirror, she was satisfied that she was still every bit as attractive as a first-rate typist needed to be to find work. After some hesitation, she took Robi Singer with her. It was not right for a woman to be seen in a public place alone with a man.

When they arrived at the Café Terminal, Mór Hafner was waiting impatiently for them at a table for four gripping the Jewish weekly in his hand. He asked them to sit down, and then turned to business. He'd had his own gentleman's tailor shop before the war, but he'd only just returned from a camp when his business was nationalised. Thank God, though, they were giving out trade permits again. 'I thought I would apply,' he explained, taking the handwritten application from his briefcase. 'This needs to be typed up into three copies. Naturally, I intend to pay for it.'

They immersed themselves in a thorough study of the application. Robi Singer noticed that despite the prosaic subject, his mother was blushing. Later she admitted to her son that even then she was having some strange thoughts. She was thinking that this man could easily be courting her, and the regulars at the café, and the waiters, must be thinking the same thing. Of course, with his balding head and baggy eyes he'd make a pretty elderly suitor, more than twenty years her senior, but at least he was *there*. And when it came time to pay the bill, and Robi's mother made a show of rejecting Mr Hafner's offer to pay for her espresso and her son's raspberry soda, she was elated when he wouldn't hear of it. It was the first time in many years that a man was picking up the tab for her.

A week later, when Robi Singer came home from the orphanage, his mother said, 'Guess what? I have someone.' There was a twinkle in her eye, but a trace of apprehension in her voice. She made Robi swear solemnly that in the presence of Grandmother he wouldn't so much as hint at the existence of Mór Hafner. 'Let this be our little secret,' she said ingratiatingly.

At first, Robi Singer was glad to share a secret with his mother. He liked being in cahoots with her. When Mother brought home the money she'd earned for the typing, for instance, they exchanged a knowing look. The tailor hadn't known that the typist, who had been so earnestly recommended to him, was out of practice. It had taken her three evenings to come up with an acceptable copy.

'This Hafner of yours,' Grandmother said innocently, 'is a miser.'

Little did she know that her comment cut her daughter to the quick. 'He wanted to give me more, but I wouldn't take it,' she said, and her face turned crimson.

'I like you.' According to the way Mother told it, Hafner's first declaration was this simple, 'I like you.' Then the brand-new suitor quickly added, 'Of course, you mustn't expect too much of me. I'm married.'

'Just my luck,' Mother sighed, not for the first time. 'Any man worth his salt is already married.'

To set up a time to meet, either Hafner called the Bureau for Textile Exports, or Mother called Forge Ahead. Their first meetings, which Mother called platonic, were spent strolling for an hour or two in the afternoon along the banks of the Danube. This was as much as Hafner could get away with at home. They didn't dare go to Margaret Island, because they were bound to run into Mother's friends. If the weather was cool, or if it rained, they went to a café in Buda. By then Uncle Móric was no longer as liberal as he'd been the first time, and he let Robi's mother pay for her coffee. Obviously, he had to account for his money as well as his time.

Mother said that these riverside chats were spent trying to clarify their relationship. For her part, Mother insisted that without mutual attraction it was impossible to go to bed with someone, a view she'd shared with her son more than once. While for his part, and with reference to a long life's experience, Mór Hafner said that without going to bed, the attraction Mother was talking about would never materialise in the first place. 'Love begins in the head and ends in the bedroom,' he'd say, laughing heartily at his own witticism.

Robi Singer was itching to know more about what it meant 'to go to bed', what it was like when two grownups loved each other, and what part the bed, mentioned by Uncle Móric with such good cheer, had to play in all this. But he didn't have the nerve to ask his mother. Instead, empowered by their shared secret, he merely asked her if Hafner loved her and felt attracted to her.

'I don't know, dear,' Mother said. 'All men are after just one thing, and if they don't get it, they leave you. On the other hand, if you give it to them, they soon grow tired of you.'

Hafner's second declaration was no more concrete than the first. He noticed that, as they walked, Mother always pressed her huge handbag to her bosom with her right hand. 'Tell me, Erzsike, why do you hide such pretty boobs?' This happened at the Buda end of Margaret Bridge.

Mother blushed, but said nothing. She could have explained to Hafner, as she had to Robi, that once this had been her way of hiding the yellow star of shame, stopping men from molesting her with cries of 'Well, what's up, Jewess?' often followed by lewd propositions. Ever since, the huge handbag over her left bosom had been as much part of her manner of walking as her limp.

Still, wonder of wonders, Hafner managed the impossible. After a while, Mother caught herself with the bag hanging from her shoulder. Sometimes she'd even swing it lightly back and forth as they walked. She told her son in all honesty that this strolling hand in hand along the less frequented Buda side of the Danube, chatting about love, was enough for her. But the thing that Uncle Móric considered the basis for any sort of attraction was something she held in contempt.

'Neither my body nor my soul wants any part of it,' she declared.

'But will you give it to him?' Robi asked. That slipped out of its own accord, and Robi's mother blushed to the roots of her hair.

'How can you ask such a thing?' she burst out. 'I'm no common pro, and I'm not fast.'

Robi knew what Mother meant by pro, he'd heard it often enough from the grownups around him. After lights out in the orphanage, though, when the boys exchanged stories, a pro went by her full name. A prostitute was a woman who did it with a man for money. Mother, though, had her own interpretation of the word. She considered every woman who cheated on her husband, when she should have been giving thanks to the Almighty for not being a widow, a whore. But she considered it far worse if a woman was, to use her own expression, 'fast'. A woman like that was capable of going to bed with a man without the slightest hope of mutual attraction. She even enjoyed it!

One thing is for sure, Robi Singer thought, whores and fast women must make up a very small percentage of the weaker sex. He and his mother knew only one of that rare breed, Rebecca, who shared a room with Mother at the TB sanatorium. This Rebecca was so lascivious, Mother said with a shake of the head, that every Sunday she entertained a different male visitor. She changed her lovers the way others change their underwear. If she liked a man, she went and told him, and when she got bored with him, she kicked him out. 'She has at least twenty men in her life, and she even owns up to it.'

Once they were waiting for a blood test in front of the lab at the Health Centre, when Mother whispered in Robi's ear, 'That's Rebecca, the woman just going in.'

Robi Singer glanced with horror at the dressing-room door. He couldn't wait for Rebecca to come out. She was a slim woman who moved with easy confidence, and she was at least ten years younger than his mother. Her plucked eyebrows were black, and so was her hair, which Mother said was dyed. Her full lips were covered with reddish-purple lipstick, and her hair and clothes exuded a heady scent. She smiled and kissed Mother on both cheeks, then kissed Robi, too.

'What a sweet boy you have, dear,' she said to Mother with enthusiasm, and she stroked Robi's cheek with her well-groomed, smooth hand. 'Well, I'm going to have one myself.' She gestured towards the lab. 'Testing for a marriage licence,' she said confidently, snapping her fingers. 'I got myself a man like you wouldn't believe.' But she never did go into particulars, because she had to be off. To Robi Singer's regret, the heady cloud of scent evaporated very quickly in her wake.

So that's what a pro is like, Robi Singer thought. Or a fast woman.

Still, Rebecca bore no resemblance to the heroines of the jokes and stories that went around the dorm after dark. Robi couldn't imagine her in the Conti Street brothel, which had closed its doors a long time ago, anyway, but which Ambrus from the eighth grade talked about as if from personal experience. No. Robi found it impossible to imagine Rebecca, this sweet woman who stroked his cheek, bending over the proverbial washbowl filled with water and potassium permanganate, or taunting a client with the familiar phrase, 'You gave me a hundred and I gave you the clap.' No, Rebecca was no whore. Maybe just fast. Mother said, in defence of her former sanatorium mate, 'She can't help it, poor thing. It's that filthy blood of hers.'

A good thing, Robi Singer thought, that Mother was not fast. She had enough problems with her other ailments, seventeen at the last count. That would really be disastrous. She had eye-drops for conjunctivitis, Nospa for stomach cramps, Belloid for insomnia. But what are doctors to do with a poor woman who is perfectly healthy but fast? Grandmother was right. Medical science is still in its infancy, and poor fast women have only one hope left, marriage. But sometimes even that won't help, as his mother explained.

Strange that men often chase such incurable women, Robi Singer reflected, and stranger still that Mór Hafner should be under the false impression that Mother was fast. It did not take him long to grow impatient with their romantic walks, and he started to press his cause. First he begged Mother, then he threatened to leave her, until she finally gave in to his entreaties.

Their first encounter took place in the upstairs gallery of the workshop of Hafner's friend, a private tailor, as the clients downstairs came and went. When they were leaving, the private tailor kissed Mother's hand. 'I hope to see you again, Madame,' he said, and gave Hafner a wink.

That was all Mother said about it, but Robi Singer could see why they had to keep their secret from Grandmother. This was no longer some innocent riverside stroll, but a real affair, which Mother talked about with a shudder. From time to time, Grandmother sighed and told her daughter how she wished she'd find herself a man, and urged her to read the marriage column in the Jewish paper in case some higher class of person advertised in it, but a man twenty years her daughter's senior, and married, too, would definitely not be her idea of a good match. Having seen the gentleman's tailor Mór Hafner, Robi agreed with Grandmother. Besides, by now he was getting tired of Mother's love life himself. Little did he know that the worst was yet to come.

One summer afternoon, after Grandmother had just left for a Union holiday at Balatonlelle, Uncle Móric appeared in their Terézváros apartment uninvited. It was Saturday, and Uncle Móric was disappointed to find Robi Singer at home. But he took Mother by the arm, led her to her room, and locked the door from the inside.

Robi Singer sat on the divan, trying to immerse himself in Jules Verne's *The Adventures of Captain Hatteras*. He knew perfectly well that the thing taking place in the other room must be what Mother said she wanted no part of. But what was it? He kept hearing the words 'going to bed', or 'getting someone', but he had no idea what that meant. In the orphanage they used words like 'lay' and 'screw', and Robi had a feeling that they all meant the same thing. He didn't like these words, nor the tone of contempt that went with them. Could this be love? Robi Singer asked himself. The idea that possibly this was all there was to love made him sick at heart.

In the movies they never got beyond kissing, if that. Besides, in the movies, you only saw beautiful people kiss. The kiss was followed by marriage, and marriage by children. Of course, Robi knew a lot more than this from talk at the orphanage, or possibly, a lot less. In these accounts, love was some sort of off-putting butcher's work. No wonder that only whores or, as Mother said, fast women, would subject themselves to it. At any rate, Robi was sure that he would never be capable of doing anything of the sort, even if Ambrus from the eighth grade said that sooner or later, he would. Ambrus was speaking from experience, he said.

'How is it done?' Robi Singer asked timidly, as they were getting dressed in the bathroom.

'Nothing to it,' Ambrus said. 'She spreads her legs and I bang it in.' And to illustrate, he swung his huge member, bulging with purple veins, up and down threateningly. It stuck out of the thick, dark forest of pubic hair like a lamp-post.

Robi knew that Ambrus's bragging couldn't be taken at face value. Still, what he said sounded plausible. Love is probably done in that disgusting way, that's why women bleed the first time. Of course, women bleed once a month anyway. Mother, for instance, tried to keep it from Robi, but the brownish stains on her underwear, as it hung from the clothesline, gave her away, and so did the cloying smell he noticed about her during those couple of days. Also, Mother would be even more irritable then than usual. Still for some reason, at these times Grandmother would point proudly to the tell-tale evidence on the clothesline after she'd she finished the usual pre-wash, saying, 'See? Another first-class exhibition.'

Yes, that's love, Robi Singer concluded, crouching in a corner of the large divan. He could hear Hafner's wheezing in the other room, then Mother's sighs, which sounded full of fear and despair. Try as he might, he couldn't ignore the horrible picture in the mind's eye conjured up by Ambrus's description, except now the players were his mother and Uncle Móric. How dare such a pock-marked, baggy-eyed old man enter the body that bore him? And what about Mother? Why was she doing it when she didn't feel like it? Why was she going to bed with someone without the mutual attraction she was always referring to? Could chronic conjunctivitis, Mother's seventeenth illness, be followed by an eighteenth, incurable fastness?

A quarter of an hour later, the key turned in the lock, and Uncle Móric came out, smiling, Mother trailing close behind, eyes lowered, hurrying in the direction of the kitchen with a towel hanging from her arm. Hafner, who was dressed, was just adjusting his wrist watch. He gave Robi Singer, who was still crouching in a corner of the divan, a friendly pat on the shoulder. 'You're a smart boy, son,' he said. On hearing this, Robi Singer felt a strange something heave upward from his stomach towards his throat, then back again. He hated these two skulkers, and he wished in his heart of hearts that Grandmother would appear from her well-deserved rest and surprise the two of them in the midst of their depravity.

'HE'S IN HEAVEN,' Mother said between her tears. 'I was on the morning shift. I thought I'd call Forge Ahead to see if he was free in the afternoon. We haven't talked in ages. "I want to speak with Mr Hafner," I said, and a woman said, crying, "His wife just phoned. His funeral is tomorrow morning at the Kozma Street Jewish cemetery." I thought I'd die. I was in shock. All I could get out was, "So he's dead?" Then I put the phone down.'

Mother hadn't seen Hafner in six weeks. 'We won't be seeing each other as often from now on,' he'd announced at the end of their last meeting, as they waited for the tram at the Buda end of Margaret Bridge.

'Don't you love me any more?' Mother had asked.

'No, no, of course not,' came the evasive answer. Mór Hafner pointed to his heart. 'The old motor. It's not what it used to be.'

Then he'd got on the Number 6 tram, alone, and Mother waited for the next one, because Hafner was afraid that friends might get on at the crowded Island stop and catch them together.

After this rendezvous came the first shock. Mother waited for her monthly bleeding in vain.

'Good Lord!' she said to Robi four weeks later. 'If I end up *that way*, it'll kill me.'

'What way?'

Here was another expression that left Robi in the dark. But he knew that if a woman didn't get her period, she was going to have a baby, and in his mother's case that'd be a pretty pickle indeed. Keeping Hafner secret was one thing, but keeping a pregnancy a secret from Grandmother was quite another. Mother would grow a big belly, even bigger than the one she now had. At first Grandmother might not notice. Maybe she'd just make sure her daughter didn't eat so much. But in the ninth month the truth would have to come to light. Mother would have to go to the hospital, she'd have to stay the night, and she'd be stuck with a newborn babe.

What would Grandmother say to a baby that came into the world without a father? And where would they put it in such a small apartment? Also, what would happen if, God forbid, the pregnancy turned out to be twins? On the other hand, Robi Singer thought with glee, Hafner would have to pay child support. But the relatives, he could just see their faces. What an awful mess.

'He promised to be careful,' Robi's mother said, just to make herself feel worse.

Careful? Mother must have been referring to the ugly rubber thing that Ambrus from the eighth grade showed him in the shower. First he tried to blow it up, like a balloon, then he filled it with water, then he pulled it over his rigid member, saying that on the weekend he'd finally get to try it. But just then Balla came into the shower, and Ambrus stuffed the rubber in his mouth.

Robi Singer asked his mother if she shouldn't share the good news with Hafner, who had finally done what he hadn't managed during many long years of marriage, namely, to father a child – and at an age when, by all rights, he should be a grandfather.

'God forbid!' Mother moaned. 'You want him to leave me?'

Needless to say, Grandmother noticed that the usual smells were missing that month, but she said nothing, she just postponed the pre-wash for a week. As for Mother, she got really worried, and decided to see a gynaecologist. She told Grandmother she was going to the neurologist because she had run out of tranquillisers.

'Go, on dear,' Grandmother said in her most comforting tones. 'And, *für all Fälle**, see the gynaecologist while you're at it. You know, just to be on the safe side.'

Later, Mother told Robi Singer that the gynaecologist had asked her whether she was having sexual relations.

'Only three times,' Mother had said with embarrassment, 'but the person in question is past sixty.'

'Well, well!' the doctor had said with a short, appreciative whistle, 'past sixty, and what a pretty woman he's got. As the saying goes, an old goat is not a dead goat.' Then he'd added, 'Go on home, Mrs Singer, and don't worry.'

A couple of days later, the bleeding they'd been so anxiously waiting for finally came. Robi Singer's mother wanted to share her fears, now that they were groundless, with Hafner. That's why she'd called him from the office.

'I knew it would end, but I never dreamed it would end like this,' Mother said with a mournful sigh. 'He could at least have left me with a child.'

---

* German. 'In any case.'

For some reason this thought calmed her, and Robi Singer racked his brains for some way to preserve this momentary calm, at least, so that Grandmother would not catch on. It was bad enough that Mother had a boyfriend, but he himself was not in the clear either. He'd been part of a conspiracy for the past two years, lying and keeping the liaison a secret from Grandmother. If now, due to the sudden demise of Uncle Mór, the secret were to come out, Grandmother would be justified in thinking that he had hoodwinked her. He'd have to think of something quickly to make Mother stop crying for a while, preferably until the evening of the following day, when Robi would board the Number 33 tram and be off. What happened after that was none of his business.

Robi Singer was on the verge of getting a headache from thinking so hard, when he remembered something Dr Nádai had said during a mental hygiene consultation one day, when he was allowed to stay in the room for a time with his mother. A change in surroundings, a distraction, sometimes even a shock, the old professor explained, can often do wonders for people of his mother's disposition, because it makes them forget their problems. People with heart trouble have been known to even die from unexpected good news, but people who tend to be melancholic sometimes make a remarkable recovery on hearing bad news. 'Sometimes it doesn't even make a difference what the news is,' Dr Nádai said, 'just as long as something happens.'

But what sort of shock would work so soon after the shock of learning the sad news? What sort of change in environment or distraction could make Mother forget the recent phone call? He should take her to the movies, Robi Singer reflected, to something that's not about the war, something funny and preferably French. They're showing movies like that a lot now. A shame that most are for people over sixteen. Except Grandmother would never understand how her daughter could go to a French farce in the midst of such a torrent of tears, when ordinarily not even wild horses could drag her to a movie, as Grandmother used to say. Mother simply could not concentrate. Maybe they could go to a café, like the Britannia next door, which now bears the proud name of Peace. A *mignon** or a creamy Napoleon might alleviate her pain, while also satisfying her insatiable craving for anything sweet and creamy. But how long would the effect last? He'd have to come up with something more effective.

He'd try Mr Balla's recipe. 'With us Jews,' Balla once said philosophically, 'mourning and comfort go hand in hand.' Balla meant that deep mourning carries its own comfort within itself. This gave Robi Singer an idea. It took some getting used to, but finally he took his mother by the hand, and looked deep into her eye.

'Mother, pull yourself together!' he said. 'Tomorrow morning we're not going to prayers. We're going to the cemetery. But only if you behave yourself.'

It was a reckless idea that could have easily brought on another torrent of tears, but Mother took it surprisingly well.

'All right,' she said, 'I can do it, you'll see.' She got out of bed, arranged her clothes, and headed for the kitchen. She drank a glass of water. It was six o'clock in the evening. She was completely calm, and asked Grandmother about dinner.

Grandmother was pleasantly surprised by this welcome change in her daughter's mood. 'Poor dear, she won't listen to anybody but her son,' she said with an approving smile.

The evening was spent in an almost idyllic mood. Grandmother made fried Bologna, one of those simple and cheap delicacies whose smell, reminiscent of roasted meat, was enough to raise one's spirits. The Bologna shrivelled up a bit in the hot oil, and the coating, made from eggs, flour and breadcrumbs, peeled off. But Robi Singer liked the crispy coating best, and he even got his mother to give

* French. 'Steak.'

him hers, offering his carefully stripped Bologna in return. Meanwhile, they smiled and exchanged a significant look. Clearly, Robi's mother was already thinking of the next day's funeral. It was a profoundly sad affair, but it was her only grip on reality. There were no strangers at the table, so Robi and Mother munched on the greasy Bologna, which was served with a side-dish of apple sauce, with abandon. Grandmother, who had only toast and tea, presided over the renewed family peace with obvious satisfaction. Mother and Robi sucked out the sugary syrup at the bottom of their bowls, and then Mother set about taking her obligatory dose of medicine. A couple of minutes later, she shut herself away in her room.

'We got through another day,' Grandmother commented when she was left alone with Robi.

Robi Singer didn't feel like going to bed yet, but he didn't feel like listening to his usual Saturday night radio show either. He vaguely remembered an old Heine volume hidden away among his father's art notes and family papers. It contained a collection of poems by the circumcised German poet, who, according to Balla, had turned his back on his ancestors. Of course, who could blame him? Robi thought. After a short search, he found the beautifully bound volume which poor Aunt Jutka, Grandmother's elder sister, had given Grandmother on the uplifting occasion of her having successfully completed a sewing course, as witnessed by the dedication written in pearly letters.

'The Book of Songs', said the ornate hard cover, from which Robi deduced that the book contained the sort of religious songs he used to hear at the Brotherhood, come Sunday morning. Here was another Jew, Robi Singer thought, who believed in Christ.

The German poet, however, couldn't have been much of a devout Catholic, because hymns like 'The Lamb of God' were not to be found in the book, even after thorough scrutiny. On the other hand, it contained lots of love poems. Robi Singer was especially taken by one ballad about an unfortunate sailor who sees a girl combing her long, blonde hair on a rock. This girl, Lorelei, has such an effect on the sailor that he runs into a rock with his boat and is crushed to death.

A beautiful story, Rob Singer thought. But he also thought that the story would be even better if the young sailor were to moor his boat in front of the cliff, climb to the top, and meet Lorelei face to face. If he were not married, they could love each other with a clear conscience and without having to be secretive about it. As for Lorelei, Heine made it abundantly clear that she was healthy, and not one of your fast women. So what could stand in the way?

Lorelei combing her golden locks by the Rhine was the last indistinct picture Robi Singer saw before he fell asleep on the divan by his grandmother's side. He always slept inside, so Grandmother could get up whenever she heard her daughter's plaintive moans issue from the adjacent room in the middle of the night. She would then drag herself to her feet without a word of complaint, sometimes three or four times a night, either because Mother had a bad dream, or because she couldn't sleep.

Robi had got used to Mother disturbing them like this in the middle of the night, and worked these rude awakenings into his sleeping pattern. But this particular night, something out of the ordinary happened. The door of Mother's room flew open, and she broke out of it as if it were a prison, screaming, half clothed, shaking from hand to foot, sobbing, 'I can't take it any more! I can't take it any more!'

Needless to say, the moment Robi Singer was so rudely awakened, he knew perfectly well what it was that his mother couldn't take any more. Grandmother got out of bed, turned on the light, and blinked.

'What's the matter?' she asked her daughter.

But instead of answering, Mother continued wailing at the top of her lungs, so loudly that the neighbours knocked on the wall.

Perplexed and desperate, Grandmother went to the radio on the buffet and turned it on. Perhaps she meant to damp the torrent of sound coming from her daughter, or perhaps she was looking for some classical music to calm her. However, Kossuth Radio had ceased broadcasting by then, while Petőfi was airing its seemingly endless report on the height of all the waters of all the lakes and rivers of Hungary.

'What's the matter?' Grandmother asked again, this time with annoyance.

Mother stopped crying, and forced a semblance of calm on herself. 'Nothing,' she said. 'Just a bad dream.'

'Don't lie to me,' Grandmother countered, with a coarseness alien to her nature. 'Tell me this instant what's bothering you!'

Robi Singer was raging inside. Why couldn't Mother control herself, when he'd come up with a distraction especially for her, so she'd keep quiet, at least till tomorrow? What a time for the truth to come out!

'Mother, I want to sleep,' he said, 'and if you don't stop this nonsense immediately, we're not going anywhere tomorrow. Understand? *Anywhere*. Not even to the Brotherhood.'

Robi's mother took the hint. 'It was just a bad dream, honest,' she said again with an imploring glance at Grandmother, as if to say, ask no more questions, please!

And Grandmother didn't. She glanced at Robi's strained face and sunken eyes. 'Have it your way,' she said. 'But this poor child needs his sleep. Go on, Robi dear, go to your mother's room. She'll will spend the night with me. God willing, we can still get some rest.'

Mother, however, couldn't repress another fit of crying, if less violent than before. Then she showed the deepest contrition for what had happened, and raised her tear-stained face to each of her loved ones in turn. 'Can you forgive me? Can you please forgive me?' she sobbed.

Robi gave an angry shrug, and dragged his comforter

and pillow along to the next room to sleep on his mother's big bed.

Meanwhile, Grandmother had brought Mother's bedding out to the divan, along with a pair of dentures in a glass, and a book, *Fleeing Souls* by Dr Völgyesi the famous hypnotist, and Erzsébet Turmezei's religious poems. These were objects that her Erzsike always kept on her night table, and would not part with, even on this fatal night.

Robi felt strange in Mother's bed. Even though no sound of any sort came from the big room, he could not sleep. He was using his own bedding, but the odours of medicine and camomile tea and sweat had seeped into the mattress – not to mention the smell of the decaying woodwork – and they almost made him gag. He remembered that when Mother and Mór Hafner had locked themselves in the room, they'd used this same bed. A dead man had been lying on the bed, he thought with a shiver. He would have liked to turn and twist as usual, but while the big divan could take him moving about on it, his mother's rickety old contraption responded to the slightest movement with a plaintive groan. Robi Singer counted to a hundred. He recited a Heine poem over and over again. He tried to make a mental list of all the boys at the orphanage. But even so, he could not sleep. Dawn was already on the horizon when he finally fell into a deep slumber, hoping that the new day would bring peace, seeing how mourning had not brought the hoped-for consolation.

'NOT ONLY AS a master tailor did Mór Hafner lead an exemplary life,' said the strident-voiced rabbi in praise of the recently deceased. 'His marriage, which was not blessed with children, was also exemplary. Having returned from the Holocaust, he lived the rest of his days as a faithful and loving husband to his wife, whom he cherished more than all the world.'

'I could say a thing or two about that,' the Devil

whispered in Robi Singer's ear. The poplars and flower-covered graves of the Jewish cemetery were caressed by the gentle early-winter rays of the sun. A surprising number of people had attended Uncle Móric's funeral. His fellow former inmates of Dachau had come to pay their last respects, as well as a number of tailors. Robi and his mother stood unobtrusively by an adjacent grave, the resting place of a former Jewish senior government counsellor, where they could look on unobserved.

Afraid that Mother's feelings might get the better of her at any moment, Robi Singer would have liked to drag her away. But she was surprisingly calm, even curious, and had no intention of leaving before the rest of the mourners started for the exit. When Mór Hafner's widow passed by, supported by two elderly gentlemen, she forced her way through the crowd and went up to her. All hell's about to break loose, Robi Singer thought, terrified, but Mother said nothing. She merely gave Mór Hafner's widow a long, meaningful look. Surprised, the latter returned the look, then passed on, while Robi Singer's mother took her son's arm, threw one last glance at her unsuspecting rival and said, as if to no one in particular, 'Old as the hills!'

THE FUNERAL had done wonders for Mother's spirits, and the unusual good cheer lasted into lunch. Grandmother had also done her bit. She'd made fried chicken followed by apple pie, which both her daughter and Robi found exceptionally delicious. They smiled. How fitting it was that without knowing what she was about, Grandmother had put the crowning touch to their little game by serving up a splendid funeral feast in memory of Mór Hafner. Nothing was missing, except the mention of his name.

After lunch, Grandmother proposed a Sunday afternoon stroll on Margaret Island. But she, too, must have been thinking about a change of scene, it seemed, because she then corrected herself and added, 'Or we could go somewhere else, like the Danube embankment, over in Buda. We might even go to a café.' But Robi was so vehemently against it, even though his mother retained her composure, that Grandmother excused herself.

'I only mentioned it because we're less bound to run into people we know,' she said. 'But if you prefer the Island, let's go to the Island.'

They got ready to depart, which meant bringing Mother's and Grandmother's winter coats in from the unheated hall to warm them up, along with Robi Singer's lightweight overcoat. Just then, someone rang the doorbell. The three of them exchanged a look and decided that whoever it was, they'd send them on their way and stick to their original plan.

'Besides, the child needs fresh air,' Grandmother said irritably as she went to open the door. But before they could be stopped, Marci and his wife came tramping into the living room.

Marci, like Mór Hafner, was a tailor, but he didn't have his own workshop, and he didn't work in a co-operative. He was a civil employee of the Hungarian People's Army, and for years he'd been making military uniforms. He loved his profession and talked about it all the time.

Being a simple soul, he always said exactly what was on his mind, and his friends considered him tactless. Marci knew this, and he'd picked up the habit of interrupting what he had to say with apologetic remarks, 'If you'll excuse the expression,' or 'If you don't mind me saying so,' even at the most unexpected moments. Or, if he'd already made a *faux pas*, he'd say, sincerely regretful, 'I'm sorry, I take that back.'

'We haven't seen each other in ages!' he piped enthusiastically, kissing Grandmother's hand. He gave Mother a kiss on both cheeks, and shook hands like a grownup with Robi. His wife Hanna faithfully imitated her husband's every word and gesture. Then they realised that just before their arrival, their hosts had been about to leave the house, so Marci felt he ought to apologise.

'Actually,' he said, 'we weren't really planning to come.'

Grandmother was equally tactful. 'Never mind, son, you might as well sit down now that you're here.'

Marci was an old friend of the family from before the war. He'd asked Mother to marry him twice and had been twice rejected, but he never stopped raving about her. He talked on about her in superlatives, even now, unheedful of his wife's presence. 'Look at her, Hanele, isn't our Erzsike beautiful?' he said to her. 'If I didn't have you, I'd marry her in no time, if you'll excuse the expression.' Hanele was nodding her enthusiastic support.

Then Marci turned to Grandmother, and launched into a discourse on the problems he was facing at work. 'Don't tell anyone, Madame, but we have an urgent order for new uniforms,' he said. 'The Germans are arming themselves – at least, half of them are – so we need the uniforms, if you don't mind me saying so.'

Robi Singer wanted to steer the conversation away from tailoring. Since he couldn't think of anything else, he launched into a discourse on the Romans and the countless wars they'd waged against the Jews. Bar Kochba had beaten them at every turn, and it was a shame he'd fallen later in battle.

'The child is very smart, *umberufen*,'* Marci noted much impressed. 'What do you want to be when you grow up?'

'An art historian,' Robi said proudly. He was feeling much relieved, now that at last the conversation had been steered away from Marci's dangerous occupation.

'That's what I call a profession!' Marci said enthusiastically. 'Your poor father wanted to be an art historian, too. A shame he didn't make it. But if you can't

---

* Yiddish. Much used throughout Central Europe. It means 'God forbid'. A deprecation to ward off evil.

say anything good about the dead, don't say anything at all, that's my motto.'

This comment was followed by a long, respectful silence broken by Marci. 'Poor Bar Kochba, too,' he sighed, 'now there was another *Pechvogel* if ever there was one!' Then, possibly feeling that the terrain of history was too much like a boggy marsh, he turned back to the present. 'Such a lot of people die these days,' he said, giving a significant look around.

Robi Singer shot an apprehensive look at Mother, then began questioning Uncle Marci about what was happening in the Army. Would there be war? Robi felt that he couldn't have hit upon a more innocent subject, if he'd tried.

'Curiosity killed the cat,' Marci threatened jocularly, wagging a finger. 'For one thing, that's a military secret, Robi dear. For another, nobody knows.' And having said that, Uncle Marci quickly turned back to the subject he'd brought up a moment ago. 'Enough people are dying even without a war,' he said, turning to his wife for affirmation. 'Isn't that so, Hanele? Poor Hafner, for one.'

Hanele nodded her agreement.

'Poor Hafner. He was just buried yesterday. We almost went to the funeral ourselves.'

For a moment, Mother lost her self-control. 'Did you know him?' she asked with signs of emotional overload.

'Naturally,' Marci said. 'We all know each other in the profession. Why do you ask, Erzsi, dear? Did you know him, too?'

'No, of course not,' Mother said, recovering herself. But her fingers dug deep into the sides of the armchair.

In the ensuing silence, Grandmother made a great effort to search her memory for the familiar-sounding name. 'Ah!' she said, turning to her daughter, 'I know. Wasn't he the Hafner, the one that was such a *Dreckfresser*?* The one who had the nerve to pay you twenty-one forints for all that work?'

---

* Yiddish, *colloq.*, *lit.* 'shit eater, tight arse.'

Mother was at a loss for an answer, and Grandmother must have felt something, because she proceeded to shove Mór Hafner right back into the hidden recesses of her memory, where she'd just now unearthed him. 'If you can't say anything good about the dead,' she said, it being her turn to put an end to the subject, 'it's best to say nothing at all.'

Even the notoriously tactless Marci understood that for some reason, he was ill advised to bring up death and tailors that particular afternoon. 'I saw a Fernandel film last week,' he announced with an outpouring of enthusiasm, and he launched into a detailed account of the saucy French story. 'A young man climbs through the window to this woman's room, and they make a child in the dark...'

'Tut, tut, Marci,' Grandmother interrupted, 'subjects like that are *nicht vor dem Kind*.'* She shook her head disapprovingly, although she clearly enjoyed the story that was not for the ears of children, and in which Fernandel, who played the boy's father, didn't know what to do with the grandchild that Heaven saw fit to drop in his lap. Marci told the story from beginning to end in minute detail, and he acted out the comic situations and even did an uncanny imitation of Fernandel. Everyone present, including Uncle Marci himself, was screaming with laughter. Mother laughed, too, loudly and from the heart, so that it brought tears to her eyes – a lucky thing, because that way nobody realised just when Mother's light-hearted laughter had turned to bitter tears.

'*Sh'ma Yisroel!*' Marci said, sincerely contrite. 'How can I be so tactless? Please excuse me. Forget what I said.'

Meanwhile, Hanele was looking around in alarm, searching for a safe spot to rest her eyes, and they fell on the window. 'It gets dark early this time of the year,' she said, giving Marci a meaningful glance. She stood up and grabbed her husband by the arm, and they made a panicky retreat to the hall.

* German 'Not for the children'.

'SO MUCH FOR THEM,' Grandmother said after she saw the frightened couple to the door. 'They won't be showing up here again any time soon.' Then she turned to her daughter and grandson. 'You're keeping something from me. I want to know what it is.'

But she didn't get an answer. Robi Singer was concentrating all his energies on avoiding Mother's eyes, and Mother was still holding on to the arm of her chair for dear life as the tears came streaming down her face.

'Go on, you can tell me,' Grandmother urged, and she decided to show her hand. 'You didn't go to the service this morning,' she said. 'You don't get mud and grass stuck on your shoes from prayers.'

It seemed to Robi Singer that the fragile shell of silence that had preserved Mother's secret for so long was about to burst. He thought Mother would now make a clean breast of things.

'What happened is,' Mother began, breaking the silence, and Robi could almost hear her say, 'What happened was that my lover died. He was sixty-three and married and we attended the funeral and now I'm mourning him. I can mourn whoever I want.' That was the declaration Robi expected to hear, after which you could only dic, or exactly the opposite, start a new life free of lies, and with sincere gratitude for the exquisite world of the Jewish or Christian God, the way other, normal people do. Just a couple of sentences like that, and Robi Singer would have thrown his arms around Mother. But that wasn't what happened.

'What happened is...' Mother began. But she never got past those three words, because she got such a bad case of the hiccups, she couldn't breathe.

Frightened and concerned, Grandmother tried to soothe her. 'Don't say anything! Just don't say anything!'

Of course, by then Mother couldn't have said anything had she tried. This spastic, gagging rattle in her throat was her last desperate attempt to keep back the name she would not speak, the two words that were all that was left to her of the last man in her life, for whose sake she'd still get her hair permed now and then and wear her red butterfly frock when they went on walks along the shores of the river Danube.

'GO AND GET THE DOCTOR,' Grandmother said to Robi Singer, when she saw her daughter's hiccups would not let up, not even after three glasses of water.

At the Szondi Street Health Centre the old, asthmatic Dr Sigrai was on duty.

'What is it this time, son?' he asked, with evident lack of enthusiasm.

'My mother, Sir. She's got the hiccups, and she can't breathe.'

'Neither can I,' the old man said, putting a syringe and an ampoule in his bag. With a resigned sigh, he gave Robi Singer a look. 'Let's go,' he said.

When he saw the state Mother was in, the old doctor asked no questions. He only gestured to her to get on the big divan and turn on her stomach. Grandmother went to the kitchen to put out a basin of water and soap, so the doctor could wash his hands. Thanks to the injection that he administered, Mother's hiccups were soon a thing of the past. Then, with Grandmother's help, they helped her into her room, and got her on her bed. By the time they covered her, she was fast asleep.

'She'll be fine till the morning,' the doctor said. 'But first thing tomorrow, take her to a neurologist. I'm no expert, but it seems to me she's up for another sleeping cure.'

He refused to take the money Grandmother tried to give him as a sign of her appreciation. 'It's not money I need,

Madame,' he growled at her, 'but good health. Give me good health, if you can.'

IT WAS FIVE in the afternoon, and Robi Singer had to be on the Number 33 tram by six if he wanted to make it to Zichy Street by seven. Now that there was peace and quiet, Grandmother sat down by the sewing machine borrowed from the congregation so she could turn the frayed lapel of Robi Singer's blue shirt inside out and repair his reddish-brown corduroys with the hole in the seat. Grandmother was a true artist when it came to repairs of that sort. She rescued shirts, slacks and jumpers that others would have thrown out a long time ago. 'There are no hopeless clothes,' she used to say, in appreciation of her own expertise, 'just bad seamstresses.' She also had an uncanny gift for darning socks.

Grandmother sat with her back to Robi Singer, working the sewing machine with her foot, while Robi was going through the Heine volume at the dining table. Just then, he thought he heard a strange new sound mingling with the rhythmic drone of the sewing machine, a high, thin, staccato sound. When the sewing machine fell silent, possibly because Grandmother had to fix the needle, the unfamiliar sound could be heard on its own, more distinct and forceful than before. Robi Singer was shocked. Grandmother was crying.

What's going on today? Robi Singer thought. What's this? The day of tears and woe? He held back his breath as he listened to the sobbing that was growing quickly into a plaintive howl. That was something he'd come to expect from Mother, but coming from Grandmother, it was strange and unsettling. Grandmother never cried, at least, not since he'd known her; she might have cried earlier, during the war, the first or the second, but even then, silently. She would have never lost her dignity. Grownups shouldn't cry,

Robi thought, it's an admission of weakness. Robi Singer couldn't remember the last time he'd cried himself. Maybe it had happened when he was very little, maybe a baby, but probably not even then. He was losing his patience.

'What's the matter, Grandmother?' he asked.

Grandmother remained seated by the sewing machine. Then she turned halfway around so that Robi could see her tear-stained face, then softly, distinctly, she said, 'I can't take it any more. I can't live in the same apartment as your mother any more.'

4

'IF ONLY YOU had someone,' Grandmother kept saying to her daughter with a sad sigh. 'Also, the child could use a father,' she said, with almost the same emphasis she used when talking about her grandson's increasingly urgent need for a real winter coat. Except, buying a winter coat was contingent on just one thing: whether Grandmother would get the bonus she'd been waiting for from the Kerchief-dyers' Co-operative. Finding a new husband for Mother and a father for him was altogether different, Robi Singer was thinking, as he headed for Óbuda on the Number 33 tram. The light snow was slowly covering the streets of Angels' Land, the conductor inside the car had dozed off, and the tram was nearly empty.

The question was, would Grandmother really want a new member in the family who would be her daughter's husband, Robi's stepfather, and her son-in-law? Robi Singer couldn't help feeling that his grandmother would have mixed emotions about such a man. She kept encouraging Mother to find herself a good man from the pick in the Jewish paper, but in the presence of friends and relations, she'd praise her for remaining faithful to her dead husband, and she'd even add that she'd never find the likes of poor Bandi again anyway.

Robi concluded that this sort of faithfulness beyond the grave must be a family trait. Mother must have inherited it – or the tendency at any rate – from Grandmother, because Grandmother said that traits couldn't be inherited, only tendencies. Grandmother didn't get married again either, after the First World War, when her husband disappeared in Siberia. Of course, she'd kept on hoping, year after year, that Grandfather would come home. Being dead and being unaccounted for were not the same thing. Besides, a miracle could always happen. Grandfather might still appear one day from the cold Siberian shadowlands, ringing their doorbell, causing not only joyous surprise but a number of problems. First and foremost, where would they put him? Obviously, he'd end up sleeping with Grandmother on the big divan, but in that case, they'd need to find a bed for Robi in a hurry. That was something they'd been mulling over for some time now anyway, because Grandmother said it wasn't healthy for an adolescent boy to sleep in a bed with a grown woman, even if she did happen to be his grandmother.

Apart from the ever-shrinking likelihood of Grandfather appearing at their door after thirty-eight years as a POW, Grandmother had had another reason for not getting married a second time. She could have had a suitor for every finger on both hands, as she said, but she was thinking of her daughter, and she concluded that it was better for her to stay half-orphaned than be stuck with a bad stepfather. She later came to regret her decision. She should have slept on it, she said.

After all, there was no law against a good husband making a good stepfather. Besides, it would have been much easier for two to bring up a child than for one. But no use crying over spilt milk.

Just like the brace, Robi Singer thought. Soon after Mother was born, the celebrated specialist Dr Báron had strongly recommended the use of a brace to correct her dislocated hip. Grandmother bought one for her, except she'd taken it off every time the baby howled in protest, which never failed to happen whenever Grandmother tried to put it on.

'And now she's walking with a limp, poor dear,' Grandmother lamented, 'and it's probably too late now anyway for her to find a husband. But when you grow up, Robi dear,' she added with a serene, otherworldly expression on her face, 'you will find yourself a beautiful and good wife worthy of a learned art historian. You will have several children and a big apartment with central heating, even a bathroom. You will find true happiness. A pity I won't be there to see it.'

'Yes, that soft-heartedness with the brace was a mistake,' Grandmother said to Robi Singer, 'but your mother's childhood was idyllic, and so were her teenage years. I cooked her food, I washed her clothes, I ironed her things. She always looked neat, she ate properly, and I didn't mind her having friends over. You have no idea how many children are neglected by their parents, and then they have to grow up on the street, poor things. But my poor Erzsike never lacked for anything.'

Let's face it, Robi Singer thought, Grandmother is still caring for Mother like she used to. She puts out her clothes on the chair every night, so she won't have to rush in the morning. Mother doesn't have to raise a finger at home, and it's been like this for over forty years. Grandmother isn't kidding when she says she's sacrificed her life for her daughter.

ROBI SINGER'S mother often thought of ways to show her gratitude for all this loving care. Once Grandmother was taking a holiday at Lake Balaton, and they were expecting her home on the Sunday afternoon train. Mother decided to welcome her with supper. Early Saturday morning she went to the Lehel Square market, and bought a whole chicken, two pounds of grade A potatoes, and three Napoleons from the Hotel Béke pastry shop. Instead of going to the service on Sunday, she spent the entire morning cooking.

If good intentions could work miracles, this hot meal would have been a gourmet's delight. But it wasn't. The fried chicken as the second course couldn't make up for the vegetable soup, which had neither vegetables nor salt. The coating on the chicken was burnt coal black, and the meat inside remained pink and bloody. The potatoes, which were the contribution of Robi Singer's hands, were nearly edible, except for that sudden, inadvertent movement with the salt shaker. It was a crying shame.

As a result, Grandmother just nibbled on the holiday dinner made in her honour. But she couldn't resist the Napoleons, and they did her in. The pastry looked delicious to the eye, but it must have stood too long in the cool pantry. As Grandmother tactfully put it, it tasted a bit stale.

Half an hour later, Grandmother lay on the divan in spasms. What a scare! Luckily, the laxatives did the trick, and after running out of the room a number of times, Grandmother felt much relieved. She even made a little joke. 'This time,' she said, 'you almost managed to poison me.'

Mother was disconsolate. She was worthless. She couldn't walk up the stairs or down the stairs, she couldn't type, she couldn't play the piano, she couldn't even make dinner.

'I'm such a mess,' she sobbed, 'I'm such a mess!'

Drawing her close, Grandmother kissed her. 'Never you mind,' she said. 'At least this way, I have you all to myself.'

'SHE ALSO PLAYED the piano beautifully, poor thing,' Grandmother went on. 'I rented her a small piano. She played Verdi operas. Our relatives were in awe of her. She had a happy childhood. Her days were filled with music. She had no cause for complaint.'

Robi Singer envied his mother for all that music. There's nothing like music, he reflected as the Number 33 tram headed from Marx Square towards Stalin Bridge. He wasn't thinking of the music you hear on the radio in passing, but real music, the kind they played in concert halls and the Opera. The Opera, especially. Robi Singer was proud of the fact that he was well versed in music. He knew the contents of all the Verdi operas, which his teacher Mrs Oszwald used to recite to them during their free period. Robi Singer was really sorry that he'd never heard a single note of these illustrious musical pieces.

Still, even without the music, he could feel the murky twilight recesses that stir the soul. He could see Gilda's bleeding body in the sack and Azucena at the stake; he could feel the horror of Radames and Aida's death in the crypt beneath the temple; and he made up his mind that when he grew up he'd go to the Opera at least once. Or maybe the Erkel, though Mrs Oszwald had warned him against it, saying that its acoustics were not up to standard.

'In short, your mother had a happy and satisfying childhood,' Grandmother went on. 'She didn't become a concert pianist, because they wouldn't take Jews at the Music Academy, and I made her stop practising, of course. But she learned to type and take shorthand, which was a good profession back then for the daughter of a war widow. And with time she got to like it, especially in summer, which she spent with Aunt Jutka and Uncle Eugene in Miskolctapolca, may they rest in peace, because she didn't have to type then. They never came back from Auschwitz, my poor beloved sister, while your Uncle Eugene, he was the best engineer in town, a real intellectual, so you can imagine, Robi dear, how they spoiled her. They loved her more than their own son, practically, poor Zoltán, may he rest in peace. But where was I? Oh, yes. I was talking about happiness.'

And that wasn't all. According to her own account, Grandmother also played the lion's share in finding such a good match for her daughter. Bandi was no ordinary man. He was an art historian, he needed special consideration. Just before the wedding, for instance, he announced that he wrote his studies in a café, where he had his own table, and he spent his nights there. Grandmother knew that writers were an odd lot, but she didn't think it right that a new wife should be left to fend for herself in the evening.

'You know what, son?' she'd said, cutting the Gordian knot. 'I'll make you all the coffee you want right here at home, and you'll sit down by the desk and write. At least you won't be distracted.'

And that's how it was. After the wedding, Andor Singer never left his wife's side until he was called in for forced labour service, and all that survived as a reminder of all that heavy coffee drinking was a pantry full of Julius Meinl coffee tins marked 'Chicory' and 'Malt'. After the Holocaust Grandmother used them for storing salt, flour, sugar and spices.

Grandmother was also proud of the way she'd handled her daughter's honeymoon. After the service at the Csáky Street synagogue, she took a cab straight to the train station, and from there the train to Miskolctapolca, so that the young couple could enjoy the privacy of the apartment in Pest.

'After all, during an intimate honeymoon, even a close relative can be a burden on the newlyweds,' she said.

It must have been a beautiful wedding, Robi Singer thought whenever he studied the group portrait taken in front of the Csáky Street synagogue. It was the month of *Tishri* in the year 5702, the second wartime summer, and behind the wedding guests there was a sign that read, 'Temple seats available.' Wearing a white shirt and a rented black suit, Robi Singer's father was looking into the camera with a faint smile, while his mother was gazing off into the distance. Wearing a feathered hat, Grandmother was smiling happily. You could tell that had it not been for her, this wedding would have never taken place.

On a bench in front of the Margaret Island Casino, Robi Singer asked his mother, 'Were you in love with Father?'

'He was a good man,' Robi's mother said equivocally. Then she launched into a lengthy description of how poor they had been. Needless to say, Father loved Mother, and in his letters from forced labour, he called her his 'winning lottery ticket', though he and Grandmother were often at loggerheads over household money.

'That damned money. Always that damned money,' Robi's mother said mournfully. 'Your Father was highly impractical,' she explained. 'Money flowed through his fingers like water. What little he got from teaching German he spent right away, don't ask me where it went.'

When Aunt Jutka and Uncle Eugene were against her marrying him, they knew what they were talking about. At thirty-six years of age, he still hadn't made anything of himself. He didn't have a proper job, and he spent his days writing silly, useless papers on art, and tutoring dull-witted kids in German, and going to all sorts of cafés. At the same time, everyone agreed that at the age of thirty Mother didn't have much choice. Any woman worth her salt was long since married, and there was Mother's 'disability' to consider, as Uncle Eugene so tactlessly remarked. But Uncle Eugene wouldn't hear of the young couple spending their honeymoon at his vacation home. That's when Grandmother got the idea that she'd go on the Tapolca honeymoon instead – a stroke of genius, as she pointed out.

'How was it at the vacation home when you were young?' Robi Singer asked, as his hand played with a pebble he'd just picked up under the bench.

For a while Mother said nothing. 'It was pure hell!' she burst out. 'They thought they could boss me around.' They were all keeping an eye on her, she said, to make sure she didn't gain any more weight, that she was home on time, that she didn't stop to chat, God forbid, with young men on the beach, and she had to sneak out to the pantry at night and stuff herself with sausage and stewed fruit. 'Poor Aunt Jutka and Uncle Eugene, they didn't get along with each other either,' Mother said. Uncle Eugene was suffering from high blood pressure. You weren't allowed to upset him, it was bad for him, but *he* kept screaming at his wife, and if she took offence, he'd buy her an expensive piece of jewellery. They were always talking about divorce, but in the end they had to be separated by force at the freight station, when they were herded into separate cattle cars on a train that never stopped until it reached Auschwitz, and after which there was no more holiday home, or quarrels, or making amends with expensive jewellery, there was nothing, just *Appelplatz** and barracks and gas, which claimed its victims without discrimination, regardless of what they had made of themselves in their previous lives.'

'But what about love?' Robi Singer asked, plying his mother, thinking of the love that made Aida and Radames choose death in the crypt. 'Did you love Dad?'

'Leave me alone!' his mother cried out. Then she burst into tears on the bench in front of the Margaret Island Casino. 'At first it was nice,' she said when she'd calmed down again. Their meeting at the Jewish cultural circle in the month of *Av* in the year 5701, that had been nice. Andor Singer held a lecture entitled 'Our People's History as Reflected in Their Art,' which drew enthusiastic applause, and Mother had played Chopin *études*.

'Except right afterwards, I got pregnant,' she added, as if that was in some way connected to her piano playing. 'I had to have it removed.'

'Why?' Robi burst out, 'Why did you have the baby removed?' For it struck him that the baby had been taken from *him*, too. If it was a boy, he'd have a brother now, and it'd be his Bar Mitzvah.

'It would have been illegitimate,' his mother countered. And then they got up from the bench and walked towards Margaret Bridge, because it was getting dark.

---

* The infamous big square in Berlin where the Nazi book burnings took place.

ROBI SINGER HAD his reasons for plying his mother with questions, even if he never quite got a straight answer, because it just so happened that for nearly six months now, he'd been in that happy yet anxiety-filled state of excitement that poets call love.

It all started during the summer, toward the end of the month of *Elul*, when Jutka came to visit one Sunday afternoon with her family. Jutka was Uncle Eugene and Aunt Jutka's granddaughter. She was named after her grandmother, Robi's grandmother's older sister, and Grandmother said that she even took after her. Jutka's father was a police lieutenant and he looked highly distinguished in his blue uniform. Robi Singer would have liked to go out with him along Lenin Boulevard, or better yet Óbuda, so his friends from the orphanage could see them together, but the debonair police officer had better things to do than to take his fat little nephew on leisurely walks. Zoltánka, as Grandmother called Jutka's father, was very proud of his daughter, who was in eighth grade, and they decided that next fall, they'd send her to dancing school, too.

During that particular visit, nothing out of the ordinary happened. While the grownups were talking, Jutka and Robi played 'He who laughs last' in Mother's room. They played with great concentration. Grandmother came in, just the once, to bring them raspberry soda and biscuits. They played four rounds, and Jutka won three, which made her happy, but after a while she said she was bored with children's games.

When they were leaving, Jutka gave Robi Singer a peck on both cheeks. There was nothing out of the ordinary about this either; for years, they'd been parting with just such a friendly kiss. This time, though, the touch of Jutka's lips gave Robi an unexpected thrill from top to toe. His feet felt numb and his head was spinning, and he felt so weak that he had to lean against the kitchen door. Luckily, no one noticed, and Robi soon came round.

But from then on, he couldn't get the warmth of Jutka's lips out of his mind. In his imagination he repeatedly conjured up the moment when the two skin surfaces met. When he lay on his wire-mattress bed at the orphanage, he kept thinking of the two of them sitting on the rag carpet in his mother's room, playing the third and fourth rounds of 'He who laughs last'. He could see Jutka's braid stirring ever so slightly as she threw the dice. The soft curves of her upper body were covered by a white blouse and a colourful vest, and she was wearing a dark blue, flounced skirt. Good Lord, Robi Singer asked himself, what is it that makes a man infinitely happy and infinitely sad at the sight of a skirt or the stirring of a black braid of hair?

That evening in the dormitory, under cover of the dark, Robi Singer was so full of the memory of the afternoon that he decided not to resort to the manipulation that his Grandmother called a 'nasty habit'. Increasingly of late, he'd been trying to force a degree of pleasure from his body. Balla called it 'self-abuse', and he said that a real man didn't need it, and that sport and lots of study were fine substitutes. He also reminded them that they mustn't waste the energy, because when they grew up, and especially when they become fathers, they would need it. Besides, he warned, the habit was not safe, and with time it damaged the spine. Besides, the Lord didn't care for people touching themselves in that way. Despite such warnings, though, the older boys resorted to such 'self-abuse'. Ambrus from the eight grade did so unabashedly, sometimes even in front of the others.

Robi Singer felt bad about the wasted energy, even though he tried to reason that he was not a grown man yet and he still had a long way to go. The truth is, he was also afraid of the powers above, whether you called them Adonai or Jesus Christ. Still, he could not altogether give up the pleasure. At times he coaxed it from himself two or three times in a row, so he could fall into satisfied, languorous slumber.

Trapped between his yearnings and his conscience, Robi came up with a plan. He would atone for each night of sinning by doing something good the next day, like getting a good mark in history, or saving a ladybird that had turned on its back in the synagogue yard. He even managed to convince himself that his bargain with the powers above was actually of merit, and came to regard his 'bad habit' as a sort of preparation for the good deed he'd be performing the next day.

On Monday he wrote a poem to his cousin, choosing her blue eyes as the theme. The poem consisted of a series of similes. Robi compared Jutka's eyes to the seas, the sky, the flag of the state of Israel, the velvet in the back of the Ark of the Torah. But he found that none of these similes could do justice to their subject, and he clinched the poem with the lines, 'Many kinds of blue have I seen, but none as blue as you.' He was thoroughly satisfied with his creation, and he felt it would make a fine advance on his next good deed.

Two weeks after that Sunday visit, Aunt Rose, Jutka's mother, burst in on them. Her eyes were red from crying. She told them that during one of his rounds of duty, her husband Zoltán had died in a car crash. This happened at the beginning of the week, and when Robi came home after *Shabbes* had gone out, Grandmother told him that they would immediately go to pay their condolences to poor Rose and her family.

Robi Singer tried not to show it, but he was profoundly shaken by Uncle Zoltán's death. Still, his thoughts revolved less around the kind and handsome police officer, with whom he'd now never get to walk down either Lenin Boulevard nor the streets of Óbuda, than Jutka's future. Jutka was half-orphaned now, just like him. He must find a way to console her in her new sorrow. Being an experienced half-orphan, he could give her advice. He'd like to cry with her and touch his cheek to hers, so their tears could mingle. They would also stroke each other's face. This would serve as a good example of what Mr Balla always said about solace coming pretty much directly from sadness.

As a police officer, Uncle Zoltán had been given an apartment on Eagle Peak, which Aunt Rose continued to occupy as his widow. The condolence visit took place without drama. They sat for a while in the living room on the tubular-steel furniture, gazing at Zoltán's photograph on the wall. Grandmother said that the self-assured smile was sending a clear message to them all. It said, 'Don't lose heart, Rose dear, life holds something beautiful in store for everyone. Take this beautiful child, for instance. With God's help, you will see her into maturity, and she will repay you with boundless joy.'

Once they were out on the street again, Grandmother waxed indignant against cars. 'There's way too many of them,' she fumed. 'Poor Zoltán, too, what did he have to go and use a car for? What's wrong with trains? Isn't the family more important than the police and their damned automobiles? Zoltán survived the Arrow Cross. What did he have to go and leave poor Rose for, she's as haggard as a dray-horse? And that child, too, pale as a sheet, with no colour to her cheeks, only those blue eyes of hers, just like Aunt Jutka's, who was murdered by those madmen... Damn all cars to kingdom come.'

Robi Singer hardly heard anything of Grandmother's angry monologue. He was thinking of Jutka in the tubular-steel room, sitting by the coffee table in her best dress, dry eyed and dignified, a budding beauty, and he asked the Lord if He couldn't please transfer them to some other, more livable time without agoraphobias and car crashes, where people don't have to choose between Saturday and Sunday, Jew and Christian, and where the vicious circle that makes you fat because you eat, and eat and eat because you're fat, could be broken. A world without 'self-abuse' and good deeds in payment for bad, where there would be nothing but love and sunshine coming from inside you, so that you wouldn't have to go to the Promised Land to find happiness.

IN HIS SOBER MOMENTS, Robi Singer realised the absurdity of his feelings for his cousin Jutka. It wasn't just the two years' difference in their ages, or the fact that they were second cousins (Mrs Oszwald had made a point of mentioning when they were studying the Habsburgs at school that intermarriages between relatives often produced defective children). No. Robi Singer was far more worried that no girl could possibly fall in love with someone who looked like him. He was disgusted by the sight of the three maimed fingers on his left hand and asked himself how he could ever dare to stroke a peaches-and-cream face with a hand like his.

On the other hand, he was secretly proud of his spirit and intellect. I am good and I am smart, he thought, and he was pleased that he could admit it to himself without blushing. And I have pleasant eyes and a good forehead. Wouldn't it be nice, he thought, if, by some miracle, his inside and outside could change places, and he could be as lean, tall and dark-skinned as Gábor Blum? And if it wasn't asking for too much, couldn't he please be just three years older into the bargain?

One night after lights out, Robi Singer told Gábor Blum about his feelings for Jutka. He stressed the perhaps too close family ties and the difference in their ages. He also recited the poem in a whisper, and asked his friend if he should show it to his cousin.

'Great idea,' Gábor Blum said from the next bed. 'Just don't make a big deal out of it. When you're alone, take her hand. That's how I do it. The rest will take care of itself.'

Robi Singer had never heard of his friend ever taking anyone's hand, but he liked the idea. He was looking forward to the afternoon in late summer when

Grandmother would take him to see Aunt Rose again in her apartment on Eagle Peak.

It was a two-room apartment, just like theirs, but with central heating and a bathroom. It was the sort of apartment Grandmother used to talk about as a sure sign of wealth. Also, since her father died, Jutka occupied his room, so while the grownups were discussing the ways of the world in the living room, Jutka and he could talk undisturbed.

Jutka told Robi about signing up for middle school, and about going to dancing school, although she was good at the English waltz and the tango already. She was also learning to swim, and she was having private lessons in English. She talked about her friends, who only cared about boys, which was a topic that left her cold. Then she asked Robi if he could swim.

'What a shame,' she said. 'If you could swim, we could go to the Sports Pool on Margaret Island together.'

For his part, Robi Singer talked about himself and about Balla, who had given him the pet name Bar Kochba, and also about his dream of becoming an art historian. He talked about the differences he saw between Jews and Christians, Hungarians and communists and, most of all, between the Russians and the Germans. He didn't much care for girls either, he said, he'd much prefer to learn to swim, and should he ever get married, he wouldn't mind if his wife were older than him, or even a distant relative, just as long as they saw eye to eye and had no secrets from each other. And if his wife should die, Robi said, he would definitely remain faithful to her even beyond the grave.

He also talked about Gábor Blum, with whom they were planning to go to *Eretz Yisroel*, because Gábor Blum's uncle had a department store in Jerusalem. It wasn't big, no bigger than the Fashion Palace on Red Army Avenue, and Gábor's uncle had invited them to take a look around in the state of Israel. It'd only be a visit, of course, and they were really going for the sake of the big ship that embarks from Rome and reaches Tel Aviv in five days, where they would eat nothing bananas, pineapple and dates all day.

When Jutka showed Robi her keepsake album, Robi blushed to the roots of his hair and told her that he knew a poem Gábor Blum had written, and he wouldn't mind putting it down it in the album. He had to pull himself together so he could write more or less evenly in the floral-patterned album, sewn together from hand-made paper, especially since he saw, to his dismay, that several boys had already written there before him. With the sweat on his brow, he managed to produce a legible script without smudges, and he handed the album back to Jutka with a proud, solemn gesture. Then it was Jutka's turn to blush as she read the poem. 'It's beautiful,' she said, 'I wish it were written for me.' After that they listened to the radio. 'When autumn leaves fly by my window...' The bitter-sweet song made Robi feel a serge of envy. If only his own love poem were half as good.

All the while, though, Robi Singer kept his friend's advice in mind, and he fixed his eyes on Jutka's hand. Several times he thought of grabbing it, but he lost his nerve. His entire being was centered on that hand. Happiness was almost within reach, all he had to do was to reach out for it. But how? What would be his excuse? Should he say he wanted to read her palm? Or that a bug was crawling on the back of her hand? No, that was no good. He couldn't. He'd rather carry Eagle Peak away in his lap. That would be easier.

'Why are you staring at my hand?' Jutka snapped, surprised. 'I haven't got hives.' She went to her desk and took a blue marble ball from the drawer, and handed it to Robi. 'This'll keep your hands busy,' she said with a chuckle, then sat back down by Robi's side again.

JUST THEN, Grandmother and Aunt Rose came into the room.

'Aren't they sweet,' Jutka's mother said with a satisfied smile. Then she turned to Grandmother. 'Could Robi sleep over? They get along so well.'

It took Robi Singer's breath away. Grandmother was reluctant at first. Robi hadn't had supper yet, she said, and he didn't have his pyjamas or toothbrush. 'If only I had known,' she sighed.

'Don't worry about it,' Aunt Rose said, 'I'll give him supper, and breakfast, too. As for pyjamas, I have plenty, I am sorry to say,' she added mournfully.

Grandmother turned to Robi. 'Would you like to sleep over, Robi dear?'

'Yes, please,' Robi said, and already he felt impatient for Grandmother to leave.

Aunt Rose made chicken stew for supper, and that was followed by quince jelly containing large slivers of almond. Robi Singer made a point of eating properly. He didn't lick his plate, as he would have at home, and he didn't dunk chunks of soft bread in the stew. Visibly impressed by his appetite, Aunt Rose looked at him lovingly. 'My poor Zoltán,' she said, 'he always wanted a son like you.'

Robi Singer, who practically disappeared inside Uncle Zoltán's pyjamas, had a hard time falling asleep that night. Perhaps it was the last burst of hot weather before the coming of fall, perhaps it was the closeness of Jutka, breathing heavily in her sleep on the adjacent bed, or possibly the fact that he'd never slept in a strange apartment before. He would have liked to twist and turn before falling sleep, which was a habit with him, but he didn't dare, because the convertible armchair which served as his bed creaked horribly every time he made the slightest move. But it could also have been that he didn't really want to fall asleep in the first place, for he was reluctant to miss even a second of the unfamiliar feeling which – or so he felt – was very like happiness.

The next evening in the orphanage, after lights out, Robi Singer proudly told Gábor Blum how he'd managed to be alone with the love of his life.

'Good!' Gábor Blum said. 'But did you take her hand?'

'Who cares about her hand,' Robi Singer said triumphantly, 'when we slept in the same room the whole night?'

5

AFTER SCHOOL ON Tuesday, Balla told Robi Singer his grandmother had called. There was no need to worry, but Robi's mother was at the József Attila Neurology Clinic for a sleeping cure. She was in good hands, under a doctor's care. On Thursday, another message came. Robi's grandmother asked that he be allowed to go home on Friday, because he had to undergo some tests on Saturday morning.

This was Mother's third sleeping cure. The previous cures were summed up by her doctors with circumspection: 'The patient's condition is the same. Look at it this way. At least, it hasn't got any worse.'

Mother was happy with this modest medical summary, because she was horribly afraid of two far worse outcomes. She was afraid that her white-coated judges would one day condemn her to electroshock treatment, and she was afraid that some day she might go out of her mind and be put in isolation.

For his part, Robi was a lot more worried about the second of those two eventualities. How would he tell his friends at the orphanage about his mother going mad? He didn't have a clue. Up till now, when asked about his mother, he'd explain that it was a simple case of nerves and she needed rest, because it wasn't an illness, really, just fatigue.

Robi was also terribly worried now about the prospect of the physical examinations that Grandmother had mentioned to Balla over the phone. If they were just in preparation for his circumcision, he wouldn't mind so much. But lately

Grandmother had been mentioning another sort of 'complete physical', to check whether Robi's health had been affected by his mother's condition. An illness can't be inherited, she emphasised again, but there's always the tendency to deal with. She didn't think there was anything to worry about, and Robi was obviously very fit. Still, 'it's better to be safe than sorry,' she said.

Balla also seemed to have taken Grandmother's precautions seriously. At other times he would have never allowed any of his charges to miss state school, unless they had a raging fever or some other equally serious excuse. He had no intention of giving the *goys* a handle on their view that all Jews were truants. This time, however, he didn't blink an eye and let Robi off. He even told him to go ahead and take the tram, not caring that it was getting dark and the *Shabbes* might find him riding it somewhere between Stalin Bridge and Outstanding Worker of the Year Square.

Would Balla still like me? Robi Singer pondered on the Number 33 tram as it was approaching Marx Square, just after *Shabbes* had come in. Would he still like me if I had a screw loose, or, as Mother says of herself, if I turned out to be a nervous wreck? Would Balla continue talking about history with someone who caught *neurasthenia gravis* from his mother?

GRANDMOTHER picked up her pay at the Handkerchief Dyers' Co-operative that day. She didn't get her bonus, though, so the long-laid plan to buy Robi a winter coat was frustrated once again. On the other hand, she bought the usual four ounces of sausage for her grandson, which she considered a form of personal taxation contributed dutifully every payday. The greasy delicacy, seasoned with garlic, which Robi Singer eagerly wolfed down, was not kosher by the wildest stretch of the imagination. At the weekends, though, Grandmother never made Robi eat kosher. 'You'll be eating enough kosher the rest of the week,' she said.

Still, as a concession to *Shabbes*, Grandmother lit candles. There were plenty on hand all around the apartment, as a precaution against the winter's frequent electrical black-outs, which would leave Lenin Boulevard and the rest of the district in a heavy shroud of darkness.

It was a pleasant evening. Having turned the lights out, they listened to old *chansons* on the radio by candlelight until they felt sleepy. Then Grandmother took the bed linen from the bottom of the middle wardrobe, and they made up the big divan for the night. Robi pulled the duvet up to his chin, thinking how nice it would be to have some peace and quiet for a change now that the adjacent room was unoccupied. This particular night, his mother's sleeping cure would be doing them the world of good, too.

The first time Robi was startled awake that night, he found the bed on his right empty. He turned his head toward the door leading to the hall and saw that it was open. Then he heard Grandmother moving about. Strange, he thought. Why is she up in the middle of the night when for once she doesn't have to be? She's probably thirsty, or she has to go to the toilet. There's nothing to worry about, he concluded, and went back to sleep.

But soon he was awake again, this time startled by some deep-seated, instinctive fear. The other bed was still empty, but he hardly had time to think about that, because he saw Grandmother in the dark, sitting doubled up on the floor by the divan, her hand over her left breast, gasping for air, saying, over and over again, something that sounded like, 'I don't understand, I don't understand.'

Robi sprang to his feet, and ran to the door to switch on the light. Grandmother was on the floor, her face ashen. There was a wet rag in the hand she was pressing to her breast. 'It's my heart,' she gasped, and with her free hand she massaged her shoulder. Robi ran over to her, kneeled down, and grabbed her around the waist. She was as light as a feather, and he placed her on the divan. 'What happened, Grandmother?' he asked.

By this time, Grandmother's lips had turned purple. Her eyes were bulging and she was shivering. She kept repeating, 'I don't understand, I just don't understand.' Then, pulling herself together as best she could, she raised her head and said, 'Whatever you do, Robi dear, don't leave your mother alone.'

As the inconceivable finally dawned on him, Robi Singer grew really terrified. He grabbed some clothes, keeping a steady eye on Grandmother, as if trying to keep her alive by sheer strength of will. 'Wait, Grandmother, wait! I'll get a doctor,' he urged her.

Needless to say, Robi had no idea where he'd find a doctor at that time of the night, or even a telephone token so he could call an ambulance.

'Whatever you do, don't leave your mother alone,' Grandmother said again, and her eyes filled with tears. 'She can't help it.' She looked into Robi's eye. 'You do love your mother, don't you?'

'Of course I do,' Robi said. He was shaking from head to toe by now. 'I love her a lot.'

'Good,' Grandmother said. 'You'll find a thousand forints under the sewing box. It's for the funeral. Give it to the Chevra Kadisha.'

That clinched it! Robi was now sick with fear. Grandmother was about to betray him in the worst possible way, by leaving him alone like this in the middle of the night. By this time, the tears were flowing down his cheeks. Pleading, begging, cajoling, he kneeled down by the divan, and put his hands together. 'Don't die on me, Grandmother, don't die!' he sobbed.

He looked around the room, but he could barely make out the shape of things through his tears. Everything was in its place, each of the three wardrobes, the dining table, the buffet. It seemed absurd that someone could disappear from this comforting and familiar world, that he was about to be a witness to the most terrible of all miracles, the moment when life turned into its opposite.

The Lord! It was the Lord's doing. It was penalty time for the forbidden tram-rides, the Christian services, the non-kosher sausages. Or it could be Jesus, who picked this cruel manner to protest against his forthcoming circumcision. Maybe it was the two gods, the Jewish and the Christian, taking a united stand against his self-abuse, the sinful release of the night which he'd tried to balance off by next day's good deeds. That's what he got for trying to strike a bargain with the heavenly powers. There was only one thing left to do, Robi concluded, and turned towards the bed. 'Grandmother, let's pray!'

He was apprehensive that Grandmother might prove obstinate and not show the proper humility, even in this extreme situation. But she closed her eyes, and though she went on gasping for air, Robi could see that she was mumbling something to herself. Robi fell into something like a trance, a state where he offered his whispered petition to two gods at the same time, begging them for a reprieve, a couple of years of clemency, at least, seeing that he was just twelve years old. Or just for this one night, at least, which he, Robi Singer, would repay with exemplary, self-abuse-free conduct. 'Just this once,' he whispered mechanically, 'just this once.'

He didn't know how long he'd been kneeling by the side of the divan, but by the time he snapped to, it was getting light outside. He could hear the clatter of the first trams along Lenin Boulevard. He trembled as he raised his eyes, but when he did, he saw Grandmother sitting up in bed, breathing steadily. She looked almost her old self. 'Poor child, what a scare I gave you,' she said. 'But the worst is over now.'

'Did you pray, Grandmother?' Robi Singer asked, as he recovered himself.

'No,' Grandmother said, arranging her dishevelled hair with her hand. 'But we had a talk.'

'Who?'

'God and me.'

'What did you say to Him?'

For a while Grandmother said nothing. Then she wiped her forehead with her right hand, and planted a kiss on Robi's cheek. 'I told him he should be ashamed of himself,' she said smiling triumphantly.

AS A RESULT of the recent events, Robi Singer's Saturday morning physical also included Grandmother. The doctor put the night's drama down to nervous palpitations of the heart, and he prescribed a sedative.

'Some nervous palpitations,' Grandmother said, when they left his office. 'I nearly gave up the ghost.'

The neurologist said that, 'considering her age,' Grandmother's condition was satisfactory. The ophthalmologist said he hadn't seen such a healthy elderly lady in a long time. Grandmother could take ten years off her age, and nobody would know. Also, she didn't need new glasses for now.

This was good news. Grandmother didn't even wear the pair she had except today, for the doctor's sake.

During the morning's round, the doctors also noted that Grandmother had pulmonary emphysema, and that she should watch her gall bladder. But that was nothing new to Grandmother.

That Saturday morning, Robi Singer was most worried about his blood test. The nurses could never find a vein on his well-padded arm. They had to stick the needle in several times before the blood would start dribbling into the test tube. This time, though, the very first try was a success. The doctor even praised Robi for being such a brave lad.

'It was nothing,' Robi said, relieved by this unexpected turn of events.

Then he and Grandmother headed to the radiologist for Robi's lung X-rays. The X-rays were Grandmother's idea because, as she told Robi, it was his bad lungs that took poor Bandi from them, may he rest in peace. In such a case, the child might inherit, if not the illness, then the tendency. But no abnormality showed on the screen. The X-ray doctor asked Robi what he wanted to be when he grew up.

'An art historian,' Robi said proudly, adding, 'I inherited the tendency from my father.'

The main item on the morning's agenda was a visit to the surgeon. Grandmother assured Robi Singer that for the time being there was no need for him to worry about the knife, but *für alle Fälle*, they should visit the surgeon. Just to be on the safe side. When they were inside Chief Physician Káldor's door, though, Grandmother seemed even more put out than Robi. How would she present her request, she wondered, for this unusual hygienic service?

The balding, elderly, bespectacled doctor asked Robi to sit down and tell him about his complaint.

'I don't have any,' Robi said, blushing horribly and looking towards Grandmother for help.

Before launching into her delicate mission, Grandmother cleared her throat. 'The point is, Doctor...' and she shot an anxious glance at the nurse, '...what I mean is, we're Jewish.'

'So am I,' the surgeon smiled, 'but there's not much we can do about it.'

Grandmother, who misunderstood the joke, smiled back. 'On the contrary, Doctor. We're thinking of that certain procedure,' she said, pointing at Robi. 'Poor thing, he was born premature, not to mention the air-raids. It was a *vis major*...'

'I see,' the doctor said with a nod. Then he asked

Grandmother to leave them alone for a while, and she was gone in a flash.

'What's your name, son?' Dr Káldor asked.

'Robert Singer,' Robi said, inexplicably feeling that he could trust the old doctor.

'In that case, Robert,' the doctor said, 'let's get down to business. Pull your pants off and lie down on that couch.'

Robi did as he was told, all the while casting anxious glances at the instruments near at hand. Dr Káldor understood the reason for his patient's apprehension.

'Don't worry,' he said, 'we're not doing it today. You will have to go to hospital. We'll just have a look, all right?'

He leaned over Robi, and took the boy's penis in his hand. He pulled the foreskin up and down repeatedly, whereupon it grew rigid. Robi was aghast.

'It's nothing to be ashamed of,' the doctor said, as if reading his mind. 'The problems begin when it doesn't do this. The girls don't like it.'

With so much empathy coming his way, at that moment Robi Singer wouldn't have minded undergoing the *briss* right then and there. He even played with the thought of leaving the doctor's office already circumcised and giving Balla the good news on Monday.

Just then the doctor touched the uncovered glans with the tip of his finger, and Robi hissed. 'My, my,' Dr Káldor said, 'aren't we sensitive?' He carefully felt Robi's scrotum. 'Everything's in order, Robert. You may get dressed.'

As he was washing his hands, the doctor asked Robi when his Bar Mitzvah would be. 'Next year,' Robi said.

'If you weren't a Jew,' the doctor commented, 'I'd still recommend the circumcision, you know. But doubly so, as things stand.' It was now the doctor's turn to cast a circumspect look around. Then carefully, in a half-whisper so the nurse wouldn't hear, he added, a word at a time, 'There aren't many of us left.'

ROBI SINGER was surprised that Dr Nádai could be so intrigued by art history and the fate of the Jewish people. But he was even more surprised when the doctor didn't ask him about his feelings. He'd decided that when the doctor did ask, he'd pour out his heart to him, telling him about all the complex and painful events of the past couple of weeks. But as things were, all he said was fine, he was feeling fine, thank you.

When they left the surgeon and stopped by the door marked 'Psychotherapy', Robi's grandmother said she'd only just be a moment. She wanted to tell the doctor that Mother wouldn't be coming next week because of her sleeping cure. But she was gone a long while, and Robi began to worry. Could Nádai have found something in Grandmother's psyche, too? Then the door opened, and the old professor asked Robi to come in, please, for a friendly chat.

Grandmother had quite a wait outside, but this time Robi was not worried. He found the chat almost as pleasant as his talks with Balla, except that now he did most of the talking, and the doctor didn't interrupt him even once, not like most grownups, who didn't have the patience to listen to what children had to say.

Robi Singer talked on and on. He talked about his father, who was a famous art historian, or would have been, had he lived long enough. He talked about the orphanage, and he talked about Jewish heroes, with special emphasis on Bar Kochba. And he talked about Gábor Blum, too, and the state school, and all the while Dr Nádai said hardly anything. But he obviously liked what he was hearing, because he kept nodding in approval.

Then he asked Robi if he could draw. After all, many art historians were artists at heart. 'Drawing is the one thing I'm not good at,' Robi confessed.

'I doubt that,' the doctor said, with a shake of his head. He produced a sheet of paper and a pencil, and asked Robi to draw him something.

Robi drew a house, because he thought he could manage that the best. It was a three-storey building with doors and windows, like the orphanage. 'You draw very well,' the doctor said, and he asked Robi to draw an apple and a flower. Next he wanted to see some trees, and in the end, nothing but sticks.

One stick was just like another, and Robi Singer wanted to vary them a bit to please Dr Nádai. He drew a knob at the end of one, he added a flag to another, and thorns to a third. The doctor praised each drawing in turn, and he told Robi what they represented. Finally, he wished Robi lots of luck as a future art historian. Getting to his feet, he told him the audience was at an end.

He wanted to see Grandmother for a moment, but Robi never found out what they talked about. All that Grandmother would tell, and even this only after repeated nagging, was that according to Dr Nádai, he had a likeable but highly strung personality. Grandmother couldn't quite explain what this meant.

'It can't be anything bad, though,' she said to Robi, in order to comfort him. 'Besides, being called a 'personality' at your age is pretty good, for a start.'

THAT AFTERNOON the doorbell didn't stop ringing, as if some secret source had told their friends and relatives that it was all right to visit because Mother wasn't at home, and they didn't have to worry about her taking offence at every turn. When the visitors entered the living room, though, they asked, 'Where is Erzsi?' and when Grandmother said that she was undergoing a sleeping cure, poor thing, the visitors said, what a shame they wouldn't get to see her.

To Robi Singer's delight, the guests did not come empty handed. The first two guests, Grandmother's brother-in-law Uncle David and his wife Aunt Viola, showed up with the usual dried prunes, at the sight of which Grandmother gave Robi a wink. Robi Singer understood its meaning, because dried prunes had become something of a family joke.

Once they went to visit Uncle David in their apartment way out in Budafok. Uncle David complained that he was suffering from constipation, so he had to eat lots of dried prunes. 'It's only human,' Aunt Viola said. 'Besides, we're family.' Grandmother said she had the opposite problem because she was prone to diarrhoea, and with that the subject was closed.

Since then, Uncle David's digestion had been set right, but he remembered that Grandmother had once made mention of a similar problem. Next time he and his wife came to visit, he brought two pounds of dried prunes with him, possibly the very same, Grandmother later said, that she had originally taken *them*. Dried prunes lasted a long time.

'We thought we'd bring something practical,' Uncle David said. 'If my memory serves me right, you suffer from constipation.'

Aunt Viola added, 'It's only human.'

And from then on, every time they came to visit they brought dried prunes and, every time, Grandmother said how it was the very thing she wanted.

The third guest, Aunt Jenny, Uncle David's younger sister, showed up with a tray of almond kisses. She proudly explained that she'd baked them in her new oven. This present proved highly practical, too, because, as Grandmother said with a sigh, she hadn't been expecting guests, but now, at least she could put out something to go with the lime-blossom tea. She went to the kitchen to put on the kettle, and she asked Robi to help bring in the tea service. Just then, they heard another ring at the door, and found little Mrs Fleischman standing on the threshold.

Little Mrs Fleischman was such a distant relative that each time she visited them, they devoted a separate conversation to the subject. 'How are we related?' she asked Grandmother every time, and it took a quarter of an hour, at least, until they discovered which long-departed uncle or aunt had once been a more or less distant relation of someone in the family. After a while they were so confused by the various family trees and degrees of relationships, and the unravelling of the various lines of ascent and descent, maternal and paternal relationships, that by the time they settled on a common ancestor, they'd forgotten how they had landed on him or her in the first place, and had to start all over again the next time little Mrs Fleischman paid a visit.

'Vilmos is coming, too,' little Mrs Fleischman said at the door, 'just as soon as he takes care of some business.'

Robi and Grandmother knew what the business was – another shot of brandy at the nearby tavern, because Uncle Vilmos was an alcoholic. This circumstance was as well known among family members, near and far, as the other: namely, that Uncle Vilmos was not really little Mrs Fleischman's husband, just her live-in boyfriend. As Grandmother said, they were married 'over the broom'. When little Mrs Fleischman had found herself widowed and met Uncle Vilmos, she hadn't wanted to give up her widow's pension because of her new relationship, so they never went to the registrar, much less the rabbi. 'And who could blame them,' Grandmother said. In these hard times it would be tantamount to suicide for anybody to give up their claim to a widow's pension, especially little Mrs Fleischman, who never did a day's work in her life, and poor departed Mr Fleischman had to support her, which added up to yet another case of *vis major*, to which not even the deeply devout Uncle David, who was unbending in matters of ethics, could raise an objection. Even so, little Mrs Fleischman had to find a way to supplement her meagre income, so she and Uncle Vilmos, who was also retired, could make ends meet and also support Uncle Vilmos's unhealthy addiction to liquor.

She decided on a daring business venture, and, at her age, she added with a shake of the head, she started breeding parakeets for sale. When she applied for a permit, Grandmother wrote the petition for her. When she received it, her gratitude to Grandmother knew no bounds, and she promised she'd find a way to prove it. Now she showed up with a blue-and-yellow parakeet, which turned out to be the sensation of the afternoon. The twittering little creature came furnished with a cage, a bell, a swing, a basin, sand and food.

The well-supplied blue-and-yellow present was greeted with 'oohs' and 'aahs' all around. Not even Uncle David could find fault with it, even though recently he'd made fun of a newly purchased radio by remarking, 'How much did you waste on that noise-grinder?'

Grandmother, who was very cross, had shot back, 'Look who's talking. You have a telephone. Telephones ring even on *Shabbes*.'

Little Mrs Fleischman supplied Grandmother and Robi Singer with detailed instructions. She said that the bird was a male, and thus a singing parakeet. At any rate, he could be taught to sing. All it took was patience. He was still young, so if they were careful not to frighten him, he'd grow up to be tame. She also gave instructions for cleaning the cage and feeding the bird.

A deep wrinkle appeared on Grandmother's brow, a sign that she was far from thrilled by this unexpected addition to the family. But when she saw her grandson's excitement, she graciously accepted the present. Robi Singer looked at the bird with awe. He could tell right away that the feeling was mutual, and as he was counting the small yellow spots on the bird's head, he decided to give it a name as soon as possible, so the world would know that it belonged to the family.

Robi took the cage off the table. He was just about to place it on the big divan when Grandmother warned him that the parakeet would get their shared bed dirty. Robi went to the kitchen for Friday's *Free People*, and put it under the bird cage in case the parakeet should scrape sand or food on the bed. Then he kneeled beside the divan, trying to think of the best name for his brand new friend.

Grandmother had in the meantime gone to the kitchen to make the tea. She was just about to pour the red, steaming liquid into cups when there came another ring at the door. Little Mrs Fleischman looked uneasily in the direction of the sound.

When Uncle Vilmos came into the living room and plonked himself down in an empty chair by the dining table, he was noticeably drunk. He pulled a bottle of Chain Bridge brandy from the pocket of his overcoat. 'A present,' he said, and he put it on the table in front of himself. He conjured up a packet of Five Year Plan cigarettes from another pocket, and looked around for matches.

Grandmother got up and brought a box of matches from the buffet drawer, though Uncle Vilmos was such an expert chain smoker, you'd have thought that one match would have been quite enough.

Meanwhile, he drew the cork out of the Chain Bridge brandy with his teeth. With a wide grin, he offered it around. He could safely do so because he knew perfectly well that there were no drinkers in the room. After this little ceremony, Uncle Vilmos shrugged and filled his empty tea cup with brandy. Every time he exhaled, the room was filled with its bitter-sweet smell. Little Mrs Fleischman, who kept giving him looks, was afraid to open her mouth.

'What about the circumcision?' Uncle David asked Grandmother. You could tell from his tone that he meant this as a rebuke. 'How much longer are you going to wait? I don't even know any more if the boy's still a Jew or not.'

'Rest assured, David dear,' Grandmother said soothingly, 'we're preparing for the Bar Mitzvah. The child is as Jewish as you or me.'

'I'm glad to hear it,' Uncle David grunted. 'I was beginning to think you were secretly turning him into a *goy*.'

Since Grandmother didn't deem this deserving of an

answer, she said nothing.

The circumcision reminded Aunt Jenny of her recent surgery. It wasn't very serious, she said, just a piece of protruding flesh that needed removing from her neck. The surgeon was very good. He'd given her a local anaesthetic and chatted with her during the entire procedure. But the patients at the hospital were horrible. Common. Ordinary. *Echt** prolis.

Aunt Jenny was a translator of technical texts from German at an export-import company. She was proud of the fact, which she mentioned every chance she got, that thanks to the work she was doing, she was in touch with what she called the 'better sort' of people. She divided humanity into two classes, proletarians and gentlemen. The doctor who removed the protruding flesh, for instance, was a born gentleman. 'You should have seen the way he can clean a wound.'

'I had my gall bladder removed before the war,' Aunt Viola added proudly. 'The operation went all right. But I was in such pain afterwards, I fainted dead away. Then they gave me a shot, and I haven't had a complaint since.'

'Doctors are a bad lot,' Uncle Vilmos said drunkenly. 'Not long ago they cut my belly open, when there wasn't anything wrong with me. They didn't even bother with an anaesthetic, and that rascal of a doctor nearly forgot the knife. Just think! I could be walking around with a knife in my belly.'

At this point in Uncle Vilmos's discourse, Robi Singer was no longer occupied with bird names, but was listening intently. He was as white as a sheet. Little Mrs Fleischman noticed, and she turned on her boyfriend.

'Stop talking gibberish,' she said. 'You're scaring the poor child half to death!' Then she turned to Robi, and she reassured him in her most convincing manner that they were not doing surgery without anaesthetic any more.

---

* German. 'Common people.'

'If you say so,' Uncle Vilmos grumbled. Then he asked Grandmother where 'that certain place' was. 'Through the hall, first door to your right,' Grandmother said, and Uncle Vilmos reeled towards the door.

'There's no air in here,' Grandmother said, and went to open the window.

It wasn't till then that Robi Singer had seen how pale Uncle Vilmos was. His cheeks were sunken, and his eyes were feverish.

'He smokes too much,' Aunt Jenny said. 'And Five Year Plans, to make things worse.'

'Every stick a nail in his coffin,' Uncle David added.

Little Mrs Fleischman heaved such a heavy sigh that everyone turned to look at her. 'It makes no difference any more,' she said. 'They *did* cut him open, but sewed him back up. Cancer of the liver. He's got a couple of months left, at most.'

A profound silence followed. In her confusion, Aunt Viola took one of Aunt Jenny's almond kisses from the tray. Robi Singer did likewise, thinking he'd have a bite of something for his fright. They bit into the presents that Grandmother had said were so welcome, and two horrible cracking sounds were heard. It must have been some time since Aunt Jenny had tried out her new oven.

After recovering from the dreadful experience of biting into the biscuit, Aunt Viola turned to Aunt Jenny. 'Tell me, Eugenie,' she said, 'how did you make these? You must be sure to give me the recipe.'

'I'll write it down for you,' Aunt Jenny said innocently. 'It's simple, and it doesn't take much work.'

'I thought so,' Aunt Viola retorted, then she turned to Grandmother. 'The *tea* is delicious,' she said.

Robi Singer took the ill-fated almond kiss and pushed it through the gratings of the bird cage. The bird snapped after it, and then, his appetite getting the better of his suspicions, he ate it. 'Look,' Robi said to Aunt Jenny, 'see how he likes it?'

When Uncle Vilmos came back and dropped into his chair again, the company fell silent. He poured himself another drink and lit another cigarette. Grandmother stood up and closed the window, so no one should catch cold, she said.

The awkward silence was broken by Uncle David who, looking for a lighter subject, began complaining about the communists, who made atheism the rule, took people's money away from them and, adding insult to injury, were now dead set against the state of Israel.

'I don't understand you,' he said, turning to Grandmother. 'You're the most intelligent woman I know. I love you and I respect you. But how can you be a communist?'

This was a running argument between them. Uncle David repeatedly berated Grandmother for abandoning their ancestors' faith, while Grandmother reprimanded Uncle David for – so to speak – his bigotry. They enjoyed this sparring with each other. In the middle of their intellectual sword-play, Grandmother rested her eyes on Uncle David's noble features, his high forehead and tea-brown eyes. Even after all these years, they reminded her of Uncle David's brother, the POW who had disappeared thirty-eight years earlier somewhere in the depths of Siberia.

'After what's happened,' Grandmother said, rising to the challenge, 'of course I'm a communist. You must consider the other side, too, David dear. In our lifetime, the Germans started two world wars. The Russians started none. If it weren't for them, we'd be dead now. Also, the Germans won't take no for an answer. They're at it again. Just look at that Adenauer, he's arming them! He should be ashamed of himself, an old man like him, when he was so well received in Moscow. Bulganin and Khrushchev went to meet him personally at the airport, when they're so busy. I'm not saying that what we have is the best of all possible worlds, but at least we're at peace. And also, don't forget, in the USA they're still lynching the blacks. Don't forget that! It's not the colour of a man's skin that counts, or whether he's circumcised or not. What counts is that he's a human being.'

'Hmm,' said Uncle David on hearing Grandmother's political discourse, which meant that as far as he was concerned the verbal sword-play was over for the day. Then they turned to talking about those who were not there, starting with Robi Singer's mother.

'She should get a grip on herself,' Aunt Viola said.

'Why doesn't she go to the movies once in a while?' Aunt Jenny added.

'Has she ever tried sleeping without pills?' Uncle David asked, every bit as full of sympathy as the others.

This time, their comments, which on previous visits made Mother lose her patience and ended with her running off to her room, circled round the smoke-filled room like so many blank shells that missed the mark. Then someone brought up the Frenkels. They were the wealthy ones in the family, or they had been, before their musical instrument shop was nationalised.

'They have nothing left, poor things,' Aunt Jenny said. 'The prolis took everything they had.'

'Don't feel so sorry for them,' Uncle Vilmos belched. 'They have a five-room house in Hűvösvölgy. And a refrigerator.'

'They should thank their lucky stars they didn't get deported into the bargain,' Uncle David added.

'As a matter of fact,' Grandmother said with reference to the earlier argument between them, 'the deportations, I never liked them myself.'

Just then, there was another ring at the door. 'Who is it this time?' Grandmother asked. She was worried because they'd run out of tea cups, and because she'd have to seat the newcomer on the kitchen stool. But she hurried out to the hall, and the others heard a squeal of delight. 'How nice! We were just talking about you!' Her outpouring of emotion was exceptional. 'I said, we were just talking about you!' she repeated, louder this time. '*You*! I said, we were just talking about how well your family is getting on!'

Robi Singer knew right away that the new guest must be Nelcsi Frenkel, the musical shop owner's younger sister, a member of the extremely rich nationalised family.

Nelcsi Frenkel was short-sighted, hard of hearing, and she lived alone. After the war, she had accepted her brother's offer to move into the maid's room in their house in Zugliget, and to show her appreciation for having been taken in, she took charge of the housekeeping. She was also one of the Singer family's more distant relations, but because she was so hard of hearing, it would have been far too difficult to discuss that with her.

Nelcsi Frenkel stopped in the middle of the living room and nodded a greeting to those present, then turned to Grandmother and announced, 'I came about that certain something.' But seeing that this was no time for exchanging confidentialities, she sat down on the stool that Robi Singer had brought in, and waited theatrically for the others to leave.

The certain something that Nelcsi Frenkel was referring to had been lying inside the divan for years, tied inside a canvas bag. Clearly, Nelcsi had come to take it with her, as the duffel bag she was nervously clutching in her left hand suggested.

During the bleak days of nationalisation, when Robi Singer was still attending the children's home of the Jewish World Congress, he and Grandmother had once made a trip to the Frenkel villa in Hűvösvölgy. The Frenkels had asked Grandmother to hide their savings for a while, ten thousand forints in all. 'Because should anything happen,' Frenkel explained, 'and you never can tell with the communists, if you don't mind me saying so,' he commented with reference to Grandmother's Party membership, 'that money could come in handy.'

Since then, the ten thousand forints had been stashed

away inside the DDT-smelling divan. As Grandmother and Robi Singer slept on top of it, from time to time they thought of the things they could do with all that money. At least, Grandmother said, the communists would never look for such a fortune in their home, not because she was a Party member, but because who'd suspect that such down-and-out people as themselves would be sleeping on top of that sort of sum. Since they kept the bedclothes in the bottom of the wardrobe, the DDT powder served only to keep the bedbugs away from the money-bag.

Nelcsi didn't have to wait long for her private chat with Grandmother about that 'certain something'. The guests soon got up to leave, and though Grandmother tried to detain them out of courtesy, saying that the afternoon was still in its infancy, so to speak, everyone felt that their presence was no longer welcome. Since there was still some brandy left in the bottle, Uncle Vilmos grabbed it from the table, but little Mrs Fleischman took it from him.

'It's a present,' she said with a stern look at her partner as she dragged him from the room.

Out in the hall, Uncle David helped the ladies into their coats, then kissed Grandmother on both cheeks.

'The next time we meet,' he said, 'I hope Robi will be circumcised.' He had to say it. He simply couldn't help himself.

When all the guests had left, Nelcsi Frenkel and Grandmother got down to business. Grandmother opened the divan, shook the white DDT powder from the canvas bag, and stuffed the treasure inside the duffel bag. Nonetheless, in an attempt to give a ceremonious character to this transaction, she made sure to send her regards to the Frenkel family, and expressed her hope that now that times were more propitious, they'd invest the capital spared by nationalisation and the bug repellent into something worth their while. She said this at the top of her lungs so that Aunt Nelcsi shouldn't miss a word.

Nelcsi Frenkel shouted back something about how grateful she was. But you could tell that she had something more on her mind, because she kept shifting her weight from one foot to the other. When they were at the door, she finally came out with it.

'I lost my tram ticket. Could you lend me fifty fillérs for the return trip?'

Grandmother grew long in the face, and as she dug the five ten-fillér coins out of her wallet, she shook her head in disbelief. She went on shaking her head even after Nelcsi Frenkel left with many thanks for the price of the tram ticket.

'Some people,' Grandmother said by way of commentary on the scandalous miserliness of the rich. She started clearing off the dining table when her eyes came to rest on the Chain Bridge brandy that was there thanks to little Mrs Fleischman. She picked up the uncorked bottle, studied it for a while, then, to the utter amazement of her grandson, took a swig of it.

'Phew,' she said with a shudder, 'I can't imagine what people see in this stuff.'

BEING UNUSED TO alcohol, Grandmother's constitution reacted to the brandy with the speed of lightning. After she'd finished clearing off the table, she turned on the radio and sat down in the large armchair to listen to the evening's variety show, entertainment brought to you courtesy of the state. At first she just giggled softly at the jokes, but then her good cheer gradually mounted, until even the musical numbers and the evening news filled her with glee.

THREE PEOPLE SAT around Mother's sick bed at the József Attila Sanatorium – Grandmother, Robi Singer and Anna Marie. The latter had come with a bag stuffed with apples and roast chicken. The nurse said that the patient was unlikely to bring herself to eat the roast chicken, because she slept all day long with only short breaks in between. 'It's all I can do to force something into her,' she said. 'You can leave the apple, but you might as well take the chicken back home.'

Anna Marie was up in arms against life's injustice. 'Just when it turned out so well,' she said pointing to the chicken wrapped in grease-proof paper, the sight of which made Robi drool.

'Won't it spoil?' he asked Anna Marie pointedly, but when he saw Grandmother's withering look, he added, 'Why don't you put it on the windowsill? It'll stay fresh that way.'

But Anna Marie must have misunderstood, because she raised her eyes to heaven, and announced, 'A blessed idea!' Then, before Grandmother could protest, she unwrapped the delicacy and placed it in a napkin.

There were two large-size chicken legs, quite a handful for Robi Singer to deal with as his Mother, deep in medically induced slumber, was sleeping the sleep of the just. Meanwhile, since they couldn't talk to her, Grandmother and Anna Marie decided they might as well talk about her.

'Let's hope she won't lose her mind, poor thing,' Grandmother said, voicing her deepest fear.

'The Lord won't allow it,' Anna Marie said with conviction.

'How do you know, dear?' Grandmother countered, 'When He's closed His eyes to so many things already?'

'The Lord knows what He's doing,' Anna Marie said with humility, 'and we must learn to put up with it.'

'I can put up with anything,' Grandmother said, 'while I'm here. But what if I die? What will become of her?' She gestured towards her sleeping daughter. 'And what will become of this poor child?' she asked, looking mournfully at Robi Singer, who was just about to rip a chicken leg apart with his greasy fingers.

WHILE ANNA MARIE and Grandmother were engrossed in an amiable debate over questions of religion, Robi Singer studied his mother's face. She looked so pretty now. Her skin was smooth, and the red blotches, the blood seeping from broken capillaries, which Grandmother insisted, were a sign of health, were all gone, too. Looking at her from above, like this, even her long, hooked nose seemed more appealing. Robi remembered that Grandmother had proposed plastic surgery, just like she'd had for his maimed left hand, but he suspected that she'd brought up the prospect of surgery only in order to comfort them, however briefly. If only it were that simple, Robi Singer thought. If only everything that is hooked and ugly in this world could be transformed by plastic surgery.

Mother looked very pretty. If only she'd stay like that, Robi thought, if only she never woke up again, or talked again, then possibly he could grow to love her. Or mourn her, were she to die due to some medical blunder, such as an overdose of sleeping pills. What a beautiful funeral she'd have! All their surviving relatives would attend, her former colleagues from Office Equipment, guilt-ridden, and her present colleagues from the Bureau for Textile Exports, too. Anna Marie and Izidor Reiter from the Brotherhood of Jews for Christ would both be there, and they would deliver a funeral oration, a Christian funeral oration, which wouldn't cause a problem, though, because with all the *goys* around, the Jewish congregation wasn't likely to show up anyway.

Jutka, though, would surely be there, and she'd see him standing by the grave side in a black suit and new coat, which Grandmother would have to buy for the cold winter funeral. Jutka would see him standing with dignity among the crying mourners, comforting Grandmother, but his own eyes would be dry, apart from that one teardrop that he'd wipe away from the corner of his eye with the middle finger of his right hand. But even that would look as if it were due to the biting wind, and not his deep mourning.

'Robi dear, we're leaving,' Grandmother said, startling him out of his reverie. Robi felt ashamed that he'd been caught red-handed burying his mother, who was sleeping so innocently on the snow-white hospital bed. It wasn't until he was preparing to leave, forcing his arms through his light-weight coat with some difficulty, that he noticed the large grease stain on his reddish-brown moleskin slacks from the chicken leg that, by all rights, should have been his mother's.

6

'IT IS MERELY A FORMALITY,' Rabbi Schossberger began, pushing his thick spectacles up the ridge of his nose. 'The rabbinate, as the overseers of our institution, have ascertained that the *briss* papers of two of our charges of Bar Mitzvah age, Robert Singer and Gábor Blum, are not in order, and that the circumcision has not taken place.'

At the long green cloth-covered table, Balla was seated to the left of the rabbi, and Principal Arató to his right. Grandmother and Gábor Blum's mother were seated at either end, while Gábor Blum and Robi Singer were told to sit across from the table.

'It is a mere formality,' the rabbi repeated. 'The two boys must simply make statements that they agree to their circumcision. We will enter it in the records, and with that the subject is closed. All right, Gábor Blum, you first. Let's hear you, son! Are you willing to subject yourself, of your own free will, to the circumcision?'

Gábor Blum stood up, and in a voice that rang out as clear as a bell he said, 'Yes, sir.'

Nothing to it, Robi Singer thought, all he's got to do is repeat what Gábor Blum just said. It's what they expect to hear, and they're confident that this is exactly what they will hear. That's why they must have forgotten to tell him about it ahead of time, because in order to make sure that everyone concerned would be present on this occasion, Grandmother had to be notified no later than last Friday. But Grandmother said nothing to him during the weekend, nor did Balla. They must be in cahoots. They have betrayed and deceived him. They took him for a fool.

At this moment, Robi Singer was especially stung by his tutor's betrayal. At least Grandmother knew what she'd done, you could tell from the contrite expression on her face, her lowered eyes, her not daring to look at him, her wanting to run away just like eight years before, when she left him behind at the children's home. Balla, on the other hand, was sitting there calm as the day is long, his arms folded over his chest. He didn't so much as blink, and when he spoke, Robi noticed that his voice was far too propitiatory.

'Well, then, Robi, my boy, let me ask you. It's merely a formality, you understand, but it needs to be done. Here, in the presence of the head of the orphanage and the representative of the rabbinate, and in the presence of your honoured grandmother, tell us. Are you willing to subject yourself to the rite of circumcision?'

You'd have thought Robi Singer was tied to his chair, the way he pressed the soles of his feet into the floor. He raised his head, though, and he looked Balla intrepidly in the eye. His voice sounded high and thin but determined as he said, 'No.'

He continued to look Balla in the eye. He looked all those present in the eye, everyone sitting at the long table. He saw wrinkles appear on Balla's brow, he saw the look of triumph in Grandmother's eye, and he saw, too, the shock and bewilderment on the faces of Rabbi Schossberger and Principal Arató. He saw all that, and he stood his ground. There was just one place where he dared not look, the chair next to his, because he could feel his friend's eyes fixed on his back.

He instantaneously regretted what he'd just said. He was wondering how he could extricate himself from his predicament, how he could turn his 'no' into a 'yes' so nobody would notice.

But Balla, who heard his 'no' perfectly well, now asked,

his voice mocking, 'May I inquire why not?'

'Because I'm scared,' Robi Singer said, his voice less strident than before. If only Balla would say something like, 'No need to be scared, son. You'll get local anaesthetic. Besides, it only takes a couple of minutes.' But Balla didn't say anything. Instead, he shot Robi Singer a withering look.

'Afraid?' he said. 'You're telling me that Bar Kochba is afraid?!'

On hearing the name of his revered hero, Robi Singer felt even more ashamed of himself. 'I need time,' he said timidly. 'I need time to think.'

'You have had plenty of time to think,' Balla snapped back. 'I want to hear it now. Yes, or no?'

Principal Arató turned to the rabbi. 'Come to think of it,' he said, 'it's the last week of school before vacation. He can think it over, come back, and then say yes. Why don't we postpone it?'

Rabbi Schossberger threw up his arms helplessly. 'I'm not the rabbinate,' he said. Then he turned to Robi Singer. 'Do you stand by your decision, son?'

A sensible question at last, Robi thought. 'I need time to think, sir,' he said, half-pleading. He thought, why can't Balla understand?

'Time?' Balla snapped back again, bitterly and with profound disappointment. 'Where and when did our people get time? Did the Pharaoh give us time when we had to flee Egypt? Did the Assyrians or the Romans? The Amalekites? The Germans? No, son, no one ever gave us time. We always had to decide on the spur of the moment. But you know that perfectly well.' Then he turned to the others. 'I don't know what to say. I had big plans for the boy, and now he doesn't want to be a Jew, it seems. I suggest we put an end to this painful discussion.'

It's all over, Robi Singer thought, no one is going to help me take back my stupid 'no'. If only Balla were to ask if I'd thought it over properly, and if only there were a trace of appeal in it.

But when Balla spoke up again, his voice was stern, and his eyes were cold.

'Have you got anything else to say to us, son?'

Robi Singer felt the same terrible sense of hurt he'd felt when he'd first realised the conspiracy. When he spoke, it was with rage.

'Yes, I have!' he said loudly. 'I'm a Jew for Christ!'

Rabbi Schossberger winced, like one stung by a gadfly, then slumped back in his chair. Principal Arató looked uncomprehendingly at Balla, and Balla looked at Grandmother.

'What did you say, son? What are you?' Balla asked after he'd recovered from his shock.

'A Jew for Christ,' Robi Singer repeated, knowing that he'd just burnt all his bridges. 'Every Sunday I attend Catholic services with my mother.'

'He just accompanies her,' Grandmother put in, horrified. 'She can't climb stairs, poor thing. That's why she goes there. In search of solace.'

'Some solace,' Balla shot back. Then, with no-holds-barred, he turned on Robi. 'You're not a Jew for Christ, son, you're just plain ridiculous!'

Hoping to act as an intermediary, Principal Arató made one last attempt. 'Madame,' he said, turning to Robi Singer's grandmother, 'what have you got to say as the boy's relative? Wouldn't you like to make him reconsider?'

Grandmother, who'd turned as red as a lobster on hearing the insult to her grandson, looked Balla in the eye. 'I will not influence my grandson in this matter,' she said.

'So much the worse,' Balla retorted morosely.

Rabbi Schossberger closed the debate, and announced that the records with Robert Singer's statement of refusal would be brought before the rabbinate. 'On the other hand', he said, 'if the *briss* does not take place, and as a consequence the Bar Mitzvah is not held, the boys' orphanage, which is a religious institution, after all, will be forced, to its utmost regret, to refrain from supporting the boy any further. This touches me personally as well,' the rabbi went on, turning to Robi, 'for I hear that you are a gifted student whose heart is in the right place, though the disrespectful – I may even go so far as to say scandalous – remarks we have just heard bring sadness to our hearts.'

'In that case, Robi dear, we might as well be off,' Grandmother said coolly, but the giddiness of triumph was gleaming in her eyes.

Robi Singer took several long strides towards the door before Gábor Blum could catch up with him. They exchanged a look. Robi's was full of relief and resolution, Gábor's of despair, helplessness and incomprehension. 'You sure made of mess of things,' Gábor said as his eyes filled with tears of rage.

7

ON THE MORNING of the last Monday of winter recess, Grandmother took Robi Singer by the hand and headed for to the Department Store for Discounted Goods. 'We can't wait for that bonus for ever,' she said, adding the stinging remark, 'As far as they're concerned, we can starve to death.'

The winter coat cost three hundred forints. 'A veritable fortune,' Grandmother said aghast. It was a brand new dark-grey coat, a so-called second-class item, but even after a long, close look they couldn't find anything wrong with it. A square piece of cloth sewn into the lower right corner of its shiny, warm-coloured lining showed that it was made at the Forge Ahead Co-operative, where Mór Hafner had worked till his death. We'd better rip that out, Robi Singer thought, because if Mother sees it she'll need another sleeping cure.

At the wrapping desk, Grandmother made sure that instead of their newly purchased item, Robi's old coat was wrapped inside the big white box because now, more than ever, it made a sorry sight. So, when Robi Singer left the Department Store for Discounted Goods, he was wearing his brand new winter overcoat for the first time.

Who would have thought that the new coat could make him so happy? As they walked along, Robi kept admiring its sleeves and shiny black buttons. He could hardly contain himself from lovingly stroking them. He was sure that the passersby thought he was a discerning dresser. Grandmother certainly thought so; she was clearly proud of their new acquisition.

'This coat,' she announced, 'is worth five hundred forints, if not more.'

They spent the afternoon celebrating the coat. They went to the Abbázia, where Grandmother ordered the most expensive daily menu for her grandson. It had everything – chicken soup, breaded meat, potatoes and cream puffs. Robi washed down the feast with peach juice. Afterwards, they went to the József Attila Sanatorium to show the coat to Mother.

'It's a dream,' she said, then fell into a deep sleep again.

On the way home, Grandmother and Robi caught the Number 66 tram at the bottom of Kavics Street. 'We have lots of time,' Grandmother announced, so when they reached Pest, they dropped in at the Handkerchief Dyers' Association, where Grandmother had taken the day off to attend to some 'urgent business'. However, she simply couldn't wait to show the coat to her colleagues, who were enchanted, swearing by the Almighty that they hadn't seen such a fine-looking, perfectly tailored piece of clothing in a long, long time.

Lastly, Grandmother and Robi visited district Party headquarters. The excuse Grandmother made was that she wanted to pay her back-membership dues.

Comrade Klein, the Party secretary, noticed Robi Singer's new winter coat the minute they walked in. 'You see, Comrade?' he said to Grandmother with an angelic smile playing in the corner of his lips, 'No matter what anybody says, our lives are getting better and better all the time.' And having said that, he glued Grandmother's membership stamp for January, 1956 into her membership book with his very own hands.

THE NEXT MORNING, Grandmother took Robi Singer to the state school on Stalin Road. The bleached-blonde vice-principal asked Grandmother to sit, but she let Robi Singer stand. She looked over Robi's report card, which had been transferred to her from Óbuda, and also his birth certificate. She copied some items into a questionnaire titled 'Students' Survey Sheet'.

She looked up with a smile. 'Everything is in order,' she said. 'Now all we have to do is clarify the boy's class.'

'The child is in sixth grade,' Grandmother said without thinking, but as her eyes wandered to the Lenin, Stalin and Rákosi portraits hanging on the wall, she quickly corrected herself: 'We are poor,' she said.

'That won't do,' the vice-principal said with a shake of the head. 'The statistics, you know.'

'It can't be easy for you either, dear,' Grandmother said, full of sympathy.

'No indeed,' the vice-principal said, suddenly feeling that Grandmother could be trusted. 'You can imagine. The people upstairs...' she began, and pointed at the ceiling, 'they haven't a clue. They keep badgering me for more information – working-class background, peasant-background. You know what I mean. But how is anybody supposed to turn this into a working and peasant class school in a bona fide middle-class district like this?'

She sighed, then asked Grandmother, 'What is the father's profession?' But when she glanced at the application form, it was her turn to be embarrassed. 'I'm sorry. What I mean is, what was his profession before...you know...'

'My father was an art historian,' Robi Singer announced proudly.

'Not another intellectual,' the vice-president sighed again.

'No, not at all,' Grandmother offered, putting in her bid for the school's good name. 'It's just that he would have liked to be.' Robi Singer was scandalised. 'If you must know,' Grandmother added, 'he became a victim of fascism.'

'And the mother?' the state school vice-principal asked, hoping to throw Grandmother a life-belt.

'She's undergoing a sleeping cure,' Robi Singer offered, taking the initiative again.

'Oh, that child!' Grandmother said with a groan, and in order to avoid any possible misunderstanding, added, 'She's a simple receptionist, poor thing.'

'That's better,' the vice-principal said, much relieved. She then took out a black fountain pen, and began to reflect out loud. 'Worker-peasant...no, intellectual...hum...no, class-alien, no, that's clearly an exaggeration.'

Then, with a determined gesture, in her very best penmanship, under the heading 'Origin,' she wrote: 'Other.'

Budapest-Vienna, 1986-1988

The Flea Palace
by Elif Shafak

★ Shortlisted for the *Independent* Prize for Foreign Fiction 2005 ★

The setting is a stately residence in Istanbul built by Russian noble
émigré Pavel Antipov for his wife Agripina at the end of the
Tsarist reign, now sadly dilapidated, flea-infested, and home to ten
families. Shafak uses the narrative structure of *A Thousand and One
Nights* to construct a story-within-a-story narrative.

Inhabitants include Ethel, a lapsed Jew in search of true love
and the sad and beautiful Blue Mistress whose personal secret
provides the novel with an unforgettable denouement.
Add to this a strange, intensifying stench whose cause is revealed
at the end of the book, and we have a metaphor for the cultural
and spiritual decay in the heart of Istanbul.

'Once foundations are laid, this novel takes off into a hyper-active,
hilarious trip, with farce, passion, mystery and many sidelights on
Turkey's past. A cast of wacky flat-dwellers lend it punch and pizazz,
from Ethel the ageing Jewish diva (a wonderful creation) to Gaba,
the finest fictional dog in years.' *The Independent*

Translated from the Turkish by Müge Göçek

NEW £7.99 EDITION AVAILABLE NOW
ISBN 0-7145-3120-0

four waLLs
by Vangelis Hatziyannidis

Following the death of his beekeeper father, Rodakis lives a solitary
life in the old family house on a Greek island. One day he is asked by
the village elders to take in a young fugitive woman.

He reluctantly agrees, and the woman soon persuades him to return
to the family business of making honey – using a secret recipe that
everyone on the island wants to get their hands on.

Exploring the themes of jealousy, incest and imprisonment, with a
suspicious death and runaway criminal thrown in for good measure,
Four Walls really explodes the stereotypes of idyllic Greek island life.

'Probably the most atmospheric Greek novel of the year' *Greek Vogue*

Translated from the Greek by Anne-Marie Stanton-Ife

ISBN: 0-7145-3122-7 • SPRING 2006 • £7.99/$14.95

The Gaze
by Elif Shafak

* From the author of *The Flea Palace* *

Shafak explores the subject of body image and desirability in
women and men. An overweight woman and her lover,
a dwarf, are sick of being stared at wherever they go, so decide to
reverse roles. The man goes out wearing make up and the woman
draws a moustache on her face.

The couple deal with the gaze of passersby in different ways.
The woman wants to hide away from the world, while the man meets
them head on, even compiling his own 'Dictionary of the Gaze' to
show the powerful effects a simple look can have on a person's life.

The narrative of *The Gaze* is intertwined with the dwarf's dictionary
entries and the story of a bizarre freak-show organized in Istanbul in
the 1880s as the author explores the damage which can be done by
our simple desire to look at other people.

Translated from the Turkish by Brendan Freely

ISBN: 0-7145-2121-9 • SUMMER 2006 • £9.99/$14.95

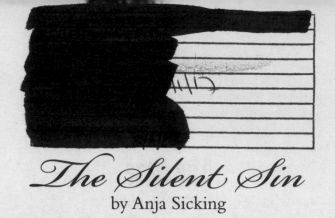

The Silent Sin

by Anja Sicking

When Anna's family – and with them her fortune – are destroyed in a fire, she finds herself alone and vulnerable in eighteenth century Amsterdam. Orphaned and penniless, she is forced to find work as a servant girl for music publisher De Malapert.

She throws herself into her work, in the hope that someone will notice she is worth more than the average maid. Anna is intrigued by the mysterious De Malapert, and gradually becomes obsessed with him, occupying her mind with fantasies about his life away from the house.

From the outside, it would appear that De Malapert's only passion is for his music, but one day Anna discovers the secret that he must keep hidden from the rest of the world. All her hopes are destroyed as she realizes he will never love her.

Translated from the Dutch by David Colmer

ISBN: 0–7145–3125–1 • SUMMER 2006 • Price: £9.99/$14.95